HUNT OF THE DWARF KING

HUNT OF THE DWARF KING

THE ADVENTURES OF FINNEGAN DRAGONBENDER™
BOOK TWO

CHARLEY CASE   MARTHA CARR   MICHAEL ANDERLE

"This is ridiculous, Finn," Mila groaned, as she picked her way through the dense high-altitude forest an hour outside of Denver in the middle-of-nowhere Rocky Mountains. "Are you sure we're in the right place?"

Finn shrugged, smiled at the small Latino woman, and hiked a thumb up at Penny riding on his shoulder and holding a GPS device. "Ask her. She's navigating."

The small blue faerie dragon glanced her way, holding the small screen in Mila's direction so she could see the too-small map. "Chi," she said simply, followed by a ring of smoke shooting from a nostril, indicating an affirmative.

Hermin and Garret had come to them, asking if they could help out with a little problem they were having. Since the two Huldu had helped Finn and Mila out a couple of weeks before with finding the *Anthem*, Finn had readily agreed.

The Huldu had been using a dwarven amulet of growth in their underground farming and gardening efforts. The amulet had gone missing after a particularly clumsy coworker of theirs had dropped it while aboveground. He insisted that the amulet was stolen, but all the Huldu wrote it off as lost due to his negligence; only Hermin and Garret believed him and did a little digging on their own.

The two Huldu found some weird readings from a particular grove of trees outside of the city and became convinced that someone was using the amulet out there. But since the artifact was of dwarven design and make, they were worried that whoever was attempting to use it could accidentally wipe out a large portion of the forest. Dwarven artifacts were extremely powerful and needed a light, magical touch.

Now Finn, Mila, and Penny found themselves miles from anywhere, traipsing through virgin forest, on a seemingly never-ending hike.

Mila sighed and called a halt, fishing her hydroflask from the mesh pocket of her small backpack and taking a long pull before handing it to Finn, who had to backtrack a few yards to stand next to her.

Finn liked the cold of late fall in the mountains and sucked in a deep breath through his nose before taking a drink of the cool water. The fresh smell of pine reminded him of the fragrance of his own magic, but more ..."spicy" was the only word he could think of to describe the difference between his magic and the aroma of the crisp autumn air.

"Aren't you freezing? It's got to be thirty degrees or less out here." Mila rubbed her hands up and down her arms in an attempt to warm up.

Finn was dressed in his usual jeans and black t-shirt, with the addition of a brown leather bomber jacket with a sheep's wool collar, an item he had seen in one of the department stores Mila had taken him to. He shook his head.

"We dwarves feel comfortable in a very wide range of temperatures, unlike you Peabrains. Comes from us spending so much time underground, where the temperature swings from freezing to boiling in just a few yards." He raised an eyebrow and looked her up and down. "Is the gear we picked up for you not sufficient?"

Mila was decked out in the finest hiking clothing they could find—a layer of Gortex tights and a compression shirt as a base layer, followed by a pair of thick green wool tights and a heavy wool sweater under a camo performance jacket. Her red hiking boots were thick and waterproof, worn over calf-high wool socks. Her long, black hair was bundled up in a large knit hat that covered her forehead and hung down the back of her head like a gray sack.

Finn would be sweating his ass off if he were to wear all that in this weather.

"I think my Mexican half is rebelling." She laughed, taking the flask and putting it back in the backpack. "My mother came from a small town in the Rockies north of Boise, so she was used to the cold, but I take after my dad, who was from Cancun, and never met a winter he didn't hate."

"That, and the fact that you might not be big enough to produce enough heat might have something to do with it." Finn smiled at the sour look she flashed him.

"I'm not underweight, mister. Just compact." She struck a power pose and haughtily turned her nose up at him.

The shiver that ran through her made her quickly wrap

her arms around herself after the pose exposed her to the cold just a little too much.

"A *very* compact hundred pounds," Finn agreed.

"I do not weigh a hundred pounds," she said defensively before realizing she was playing right into his hands. More quietly and with a small grin, she continued, "Ninety-eight pounds is exactly on target for my four-ten frame. Not all of us are six-five dwarves with furnaces in our bellies. How much do you weigh, anyway?"

Finn shrugged. "Depends on the planet, but here, I weigh around three hundred and fifty, maybe four hundred."

Mila's jaw dropped. "Are you serious? You don't look like you have an ounce of fat on you."

"Dwarves are dense. It's why we don't like water." He made a whistling sound as he mimicked a stone sinking with his hand. "We don't float."

"No wonder you're warm. You probably burn a thousand calories an hour just walking around." She shivered once more, her shoulders rolling up close to her ears.

Penny huffed and rolled her eyes. She made a grab for Finn's pocket. "Shiri, chi chi."

Finn pulled his ever-present box of Charleston Chew Minis from the pocket and dumped a few into his hand, holding it up so that Penny could get at them. She quickly tossed several into her mouth before hopping off his shoulder and gliding over to Mila's.

Finn ate the remaining two chews and put the box away. "Open your jacket about halfway," he told Mila, who had leaned her head to the side to affectionately bump Penny's flank as the dragon landed on her shoulder.

"I'm not going to expose myself to the cold even more. I'm already struggling here."

Penny quickly crawled onto the front of Mila's jacket and unzipped it herself. Before Mila could stop her, Penny climbed into the opening, holding the GPS device out in front of her, arms and neck sticking out of the zipper between Mila's breasts like she was a baby in a harness. Penny clamped her mouth shut and began to puff out her cheeks as she created a magical fire in her belly.

Mila opened her mouth to protest but cocked her head and smiled as Penny's body began to radiate heat.

"Oh, my God. Why didn't you do this from the start? You're like a hot water bottle!" Mila awkwardly held her fist so it was facing the tiny dragon riding in her jacket.

Penny made a fist of her own and bumped it into Mila's, smiling up at her. "Squee shi shir."

Mila looked to Finn for the translation.

Finn laughed. "She says she didn't start there because she thought you were a big girl and could handle a little cold."

Mila's jaw dropped and she looked down at Penny, who was staring daggers at Finn.

"Shiri shi shir!" She shot a white-hot flame in his direction to punctuate her statement.

Finn laughed even harder, holding his hands up in surrender. "I'm kidding. She said she never had a friend who needed her help to warm up before. It was actually a pretty sweet thing for her to say, considering dragons don't count people as friends very often."

Now there was a purplish blush to Penny's blue cheeks as she smiled up at Mila.

Mila blinked a few times, looking down at Penny, obviously at a loss for words. In a sudden movement, she craned her head forward and gave Penny a kiss on the top of her scaled head.

"Thanks. You're a good friend to have, Penny."

Finn watched the interaction with a warm feeling bubbling in his stomach. Penny had never liked anyone they had teamed up with, always keeping her distance from newcomers, and only talking to him. The shift in her attitude spoke volumes that no one but he could understand.

Faerie dragons were a very selective bunch, trusting only a few people, and even then, only until they got what they needed from them. His and Penny's partnership—no, that wasn't the right word anymore. Their *friendship* was beyond rare in the cosmos, and now she had a second friend.

What is the world coming to?

The sound of voices interrupted his train of thought, and he turned to hear them better. Mila and Penny picked up on them too, Mila taking a step forward to be next to Finn.

The sound was distant. Finn knew that sound acted weird in a forest, bouncing off of everything and coming at you from false directions. A glance at Penny, who had far superior hearing compared to him or Mila, and she confirmed the direction with a pointed talon.

"Thanks," he whispered, and Penny gave him a lazy salute and winked.

He moved them forward several more yards until the voices were loud enough for even he and Mila to locate.

Directly in front of them, several voices, speaking

loudly, filtered through the trees. Panic was starting to pitch their tone higher and louder as the seconds passed.

That was when the entire forest started trembling and shaking.

A rain of dried pine needles fell on and around Finn, leaving everything with a crunchy, tan coating. Finn saw the first elf burst through the trees, running for all he was worth right at them, a look of terror etched on his face.

"Run! They're out of control! We didn't know *that* would happen!" the brown-haired man shouted as he ran past, not looking back.

Finn pulled out the handle of Fragar and grinned. "Looks like we're in the right spot after all."

CHAPTER TWO

Finn burst from the underbrush into a clearing in the woods. The chaotic sight of a dozen elves in hiking attire trying to fight off five gigantic trees that were whipping twisted and malformed branches at them caused him to stumble to a halt. The sight was so bizarre, Finn didn't quite know how to process it.

Mila stumbled out of the brush beside him, Gram, the golden sword, fully extended in her hand. "What the actual fuck?"

"My sentiments exactly. Penny, any ideas?" Finn scanned the crowd and spotted the likely leader of this doomed experiment. The amulet dangled against the outside of his puffy red vest.

Penny quickly climbed from Mila's jacket and flapped up beside Finn. "Ker chir?" she suggested with a shrug.

"Worth a shot, just don't catch them on fire. I can fix this when I get my hands on the amulet. No need to burn the forest down in the attempt. You give me some space, and I'll pull the elves out." Finn turned to Mila. "You stay here and help the elves. Most of them are going to be in shock and will need looking after."

She nodded and moved out into the clearing as he and Penny charged.

Penny used a large jet of flame right above the heads of three of the elves who were tangled in a spiny branch that was squeezing them together. The tree recoiled from the flame, releasing its captives, and shook menacingly at the little dragon. Penny didn't flinch, and instead shot another flame at the mutant tree, making it whip back from her.

Finn was right on her heels, passing her by and scooping the two most injured elves over his shoulders and yelling at the third to get back. The dazed elf, cradling an obviously broken arm, scrambled to her feet and ran toward Mila, who was waving her direction with both arms. Finn sprinted past the elf and, as gently as he could, dropped the other two at Mila's feet before turning and running at the second tree, already swaying angrily away from Penny's flaming attentions.

There were more elves under this tree, but most of them were in good enough shape that they could run on their own, without his prompting. The four left were helped by their fellows, freeing Finn up to go after the last tree and the four elves stuck in its branches.

Finn spotted the leader slashing at the monstrous tree with a small knife, but it was ineffective, and he was batted to the ground by one branch and whipped across the face by a second. Finn already had Fragar out, and he swung as he slid into place next to a woman who was completely wrapped up in a branch, being squeezed tight. She had her mouth open in a scream, but no sound came out, her lungs empty of air.

Finn chopped the branch off a foot from the woman and was slashed by the end as it sprang back to its natural, ridged shape, unwinding from around her. Taking the whipping, Finn caught the woman with one arm and severed a second branch entangling a young man. Springing away from the tree, Finn saw that Penny had arrived and was using her flames to scare the tree back. She had to do a little fancy flying to avoid some tentacle-like branches that came at her from the sides, but she was more than capable of staying out of reach.

The leader crawled back in a hasty crabwalk, and the fourth person, a young woman, was able to run once Penny scared the tree back from her.

The sound of several bubbles popping made Finn glance up to see four Huldu arriving, their faces masks of horror at what the elves had done to the trees.

Finn laid the woman in his arms down on the ground and looked for a pulse. He didn't find one. He quickly started CPR on her, careful not to crush her delicate collarbone or ribs. He was so focused on the woman that when the elven leader slid up on her other side and began blowing air into her mouth, he barely noticed, only counting the beats.

It took nearly a full minute of pumping, but eventually, the elf's eyes snapped open, and she gasped for air. Finn quickly pulled a healing potion from his jacket pocket and unstopped the cork with his teeth as he sat her up, bracing her with his other hand under her back.

"Drink this. I don't know if there's any other damage

inside of you, so it's better to be safe." He gently pressed the vial to her lips, and she greedily sucked the red fluid down. "That's it. Good job," he reassured her, laying her to the ground while the potion did its work.

He glanced over his shoulder and saw that Mila was distributing the other healing potions they had brought in her backpack. This was turning out to be expensive, but what did he care? He had more gold than he could spend, thanks to the cursed armband Draupnir.

Finn turned and saw that the leader was now kneeling on the other side of the woman to whom he had just given the potion. He checked on her and saw that her color had returned, but she still seemed a little dazed. The elf leader was gazing down, tears in his eyes.

"What the fuck were you thinking, man?" Finn growled, reaching across the woman and grasping the amulet around the elf's neck. With a quick pull, he broke the delicate gold chain with a *snap*.

The elf looked up, his face swollen and red with blood where the branch had cut his cheek open. He looked past Finn at the monstrosities he had created, and new tears ran from his eyes. "I was just trying to make a place for us. I was told the amulet would let the trees grow large, like back in our home cities. He didn't say anything about *this* happening," he cried, waving a hand at the swaying, malformed, enormous pine trees behind Finn.

"Who told you that?" Finn asked, quickly examining the amulet, and recognizing the type, if not the maker, right away.

"Timmy."

Finn's brow furrowed, and he looked up. "Timmy? Like, a little boy? That's who you got this from?"

The elf focused on him, confusion all over his face. "No, Timmy the broker. He sells magical oddities. Everyone knows who Timmy is."

Finn stored the name "Timmy" away for later and stood. He turned to the trees and took in their twisted forms. Moaning like someone was in pain that rumbled across the valley, and Finn realized it was coming from the trees, not the injured elves all around him.

He gripped the amulet hard enough that he felt the edges biting into his palm.

"We're going to have to cull these three," Garret said, stepping up next to Finn, putting his hands on his hips and sighing loudly. "They're in too much pain, and the whole forest will go mad with it if we don't put them out of their misery."

Finn held up a hand, stopping Garret from stepping forward to do the deed. "No, I can save them. Just give me a moment."

"They are well beyond saving, Finn. You did your best, but we were just a little too late." Garret reached up to put a comforting hand on the big dwarf's shoulder. "We tried to convince the others to come sooner, but by the time they agreed, we felt the trees had already gone wild with the pain. It's a tragedy, but we can make—"

Garret's voice cut off as Finn started glowing purple in the late afternoon light.

The Huldu quickly took a step back, his mouth open in shock as he recognized the amount of power flowing through the dwarf.

Finn opened his eyes, which had gone from their normal deep brown to snowy gray as magic flowed in waves from the soil into him. He couldn't normally pull this much power without getting burnt out, but with the amulet, he was able to immediately focus that power into something else, using himself as more of a conduit.

Dwarven magic was unique in the universe. It was a manifestation of the physical world, unlike what elves and gnomes and most of the other Magicals practiced, which was a mechanism of the universe as a whole. A dwarf couldn't teleport or create food, for example, but they were very good at manipulating the world around them in physical ways.

The amulet was a focus for adding or subtracting to the physical elements of plants. Add more cellulose, and it resulted in a thicker tree trunk. The danger was when the magic was unbalanced, and something ran out of control, like in the case of the three trees. The elves had added mass to the trees, but the pines were unable to process so much growth in the minutes it took them to double in size. It would be as if a person were to grow two feet in minutes and have all their growing pains hit in one huge, aching blast.

It was now up to Finn to try to balance those effects. The magic ran through him at an increasing rate, making the amulet warm to the touch, and causing small static charges to dance along his fingers in tingling bursts.

The trees began to calm their angry swaying and shrink in size. It was a slow process, but the trunks were thinning, and random growths that had sprouted were flattening out. Where the roots receded, they left wide trenches of displaced dirt, making the trees unsteady on their feet, as it were.

Several of the elves who had recovered, or were unharmed in the first place, rushed forward and began shoveling the loose soil back around the roots with their hands, their wood elf nature winning out over their fear of what the trees had become.

A bead of sweat rolled down Finn's forehead, stinging his eyes, despite the chill in the air. He gritted his teeth and continued to withdraw the magic from the tortured trees. He could feel his blood beginning to respond to the effort, his berserker rage threatening to come to the fore, but he fought it down as best he could. The rage would mute magical effects both against and from him; it was what made being a berserker so dangerous, but it also limited what he could do if the rage took over. Thankfully, he had a friend who knew the signs of his affliction.

He didn't feel Penny land on his shoulder or hear her soothing words, but when her small fingers gently wove into his hair and pressed against the back of his head, he became fully aware of her. The boiling rage subsided, flowing from him and into Penny, just like the magic had flowed from the trees, into him. Her cooling, healing touch soothed some of the pressure he was feeling, and he was able to focus more magic into the trees, speeding up the process.

In the matter of a few minutes, the trees were back to their normal size, and the forest itself breathed a sigh of relief.

Finn breathed his own sigh of relief, releasing the

magic. His purple glow slowly subsided as his shoulders slumped slightly.

He smiled at Penny. "Thanks for the assist, friend." He bumped her shoulder with his head, and she rubbed the top of it, messing up his hair.

"Shshir." She smiled and winked.

CHAPTER THREE

Finn handed the still-glowing amulet to Garret, who gingerly took it as if it were an armed bomb.

"Be careful with that for the next few weeks," Finn warned with a raised eyebrow. "It's overcharged. It'll work at a much more accelerated rate than you're used to until the power has been used up or dissipates on its own."

Garret held the amulet up, his eyes wide. "How much should we hold back?"

Finn considered, looking at Penny on his shoulder, who just shrugged.

"I would start out at, say, ten percent and go from there," he suggested.

Mila walked up, a little blood smeared on her forehead from where she had wiped the sweat away with the back of her hand. She had just finished washing her hands and was using a small towel to dry them.

"Everyone is okay, though we went through seven healing potions to get there."

Finn smiled, took the towel, and wiped the blood from

her forehead. "Good work, Mila. You saved a lot of lives today."

She gave him a half-smile. "Just doing my job."

"Actually," Garret said, holding up a finger, "aren't you an anthropologist? This is very clearly *not* your job. I appreciate that you're working with Finn here, but why?"

She glanced from Garret to Finn, a smile spreading on her face. "It seems like the right thing to do. Besides, this big oaf would be lost without me."

Penny tooted a smoke ring from one nostril while giving her an "Ain't-that-the-truth" look, which made Mila laugh.

Finn, feeling like he should at least attempt to save some face, cleared his throat. "She just understands what I've come to realize over the last few weeks."

"What's that?" Hermin asked, stepping close to the group, the elven leader in tow.

"That the *Earth* is a unique and sacred place in the universe and needs to be protected." Finn raised an eyebrow. "The ship took off with a huge store of dwarven artifacts, and now that there are no other dwarves, someone needs to police their use." He gave the elf a withering glance. "It's pretty obvious that everyone has forgotten what they can do, and the danger involved in their misuse."

The elven leader, who was much younger-looking than Finn had first realized, hung his head. His long, brown hair fell to cover the shame on his face. "I'm really sorry. I had no idea that would happen. We were just trying to make a place we wood elves could be ourselves."

"Well, you have your wish," Finn said, to Garret's, Hermin's, and the elves' surprise.

Hermin blinked and looked from Finn to the trees and back again. "What do you mean? You fixed them, didn't you?"

Finn inhaled deeply through his nose, putting his hands on his hips, and turned to the three trees. He watched for a few seconds as the elves packed the dirt around their roots and generally tried to make amends with the sentinels.

"I reverted them back to their original size," he began, stroking his beard and finding a small stick in the brown bush. "But I understand the need to have a place to be yourself, and there is nothing wrong with that, so long as it doesn't hurt others. And unfortunately, these trees have already experienced what it would be to be giants. I can't stop them from striving to achieve that. But we all know they would never get there on their own."

He turned and saw everyone looking at him expectantly.

He continued, "I used the amulet to set them on a path to one day achieve that size. It will take a while, but from now on, they will grow at an accelerated rate, and eventually tower over the forest around them." He pointed at the elf. "You and your people are now their caretakers. Watch over them and keep them secret, and one day, they will provide the home you long for."

The elf opened and closed his mouth several times, trying to find the right words. "I...I don't know what to say."

"Just say you won't meddle with things you don't fully

understand anymore." Finn gave the man a smile and reached out a meaty hand.

The elf slipped his slender fingers into Finn's large grip and shook his hand. "I promise. No more dwarven artifacts."

Mila handed the elf a card. "Here. This is the number where you can reach Finn and me. If you need anything or have any questions, give us a call."

The elf took the card. "My name is Gary, by the way. Thanks, you two, for everything."

"No problem," Finn said with another smile. "Now go help your people with your new charges. The displaced earth is going to need more solid replacing before the trees are safe to stand on their own."

Gary nodded and jogged off to join his people, who were working diligently to right the wrong they had committed.

"I don't know how the others will feel about this," Garret mused, glancing over his shoulder at the two other Huldu helping the more seriously injured elves.

"Don't tell them," Finn suggested with a shrug. "By the time they realize the trees are growing too fast, it will be too late. Then you can just send them my way, and I'll explain what I did."

Garret and Hermin exchanged a look, then nodded to one another. "Sounds like a plan, but please don't make things like this a habit. It's hard enough keeping this boat running without having to make accommodations all the time," Garret said to Finn.

"Not a problem. I'll be sure to keep any interference to a minimum," Finn reassured the Huldu. "And I'll be sure to let you know about any changes that happen to occur."

"Good," Hermin said, pulling out a business card and handing it to Finn. "Now that that's settled, I have another job for you."

Finn took the card and read the name. *'Preston Meriwether'* was printed on the front, and he turned it over to find an address in embossed lettering across the back.

"Who is Preston Meriwether?"

To Finn's surprise, Mila was the first to answer. "Are you kidding me? The billionaire?"

Garret nodded. "The one and the same. He heard about you two through the grapevine and has a job if you want it."

"What kind of job?" Finn asked, handing the card to Penny, who took a look at both sides before handing it to Mila.

Hermin and Garret shrugged in unison, and Garret said, "Who knows. Might have something to do with the zoo, though."

"The zoo?" Mila asked, getting more lost by the word. "I thought he ran a tech company. What does he have to do with the zoo? And how does he know you?"

Her hand went to her mouth as realization dawned.

"Oh, my god. He's a Magical?"

Hermin laughed at the look on her face. "He sure is. And he has his own personal zoo for us Magicals. The dangerous animals in storage need to be taken out of stasis from time to time, so while he takes care of them, he lets the Magical community come and see them."

"But more importantly," Garret added, "he works as a

kind of secret ambassador between the Peabrains and us. Keeping our secrets secret and greasing the cogs that help us blend in with nonmagical society. If he needs help, then it's something serious."

Finn nodded, taking the card from Mila and slipping it into his back pocket. "We'll stop by in the morning."

"Just be aware, he's kind of the unofficial mayor of Magicals in Denver," Hermin warned. "Don't keep him waiting too long."

"Not a problem," Finn reassured him. "Are you two able to take care of things here? We have a long hike back to the car."

Hermin looked around the clearing. "We can handle it from here. Do you want me to teleport you back to your car?"

Mila shook her head. "No, I need the exercise." She glanced up at Finn with a pained smile. "If I'm going to keep up with this big guy, I need to get my steps in."

They all shook hands and parted ways, the Huldu covering up any sign of tampering with magic, and the elves working to restore the trees.

Finn turned to Mila and smiled. "You ready?"

She reached out and took his hand. "Ready, but can we move a little slower now that the danger has passed? I need to take three steps for each one of yours."

She started off toward the car, keeping his pace slow by holding onto his hand. Penny hopped off Finn's shoulder and climbed back into Mila's jacket, prepared for when the chill would set in and Mila couldn't take it anymore.

Finn didn't fight her, instead just enjoying the walk and the feel of her small, warm hand in his.

CHAPTER FOUR

Mila pulled the Hellcat into the tight space in the garage while Finn and Penny stood in the alley watching. The process of parking the large muscle car in the tight space had become second nature to the two of them. They needed to get out of the car before she pulled in, or Finn would be stuck in the car, unable to open the passenger door.

The rumbling motor purred one final time before settling down for the night, the pinging sound of cooling metal like wind chimes in the garage. Mila opened the driver's door and climbed out wearily.

"I swear my ass is going to fall off," she complained, rubbing an ass cheek with the heel of her hand. "I haven't hiked that far since college."

"I could rub it if it would make you feel better," Finn offered.

Penny smacked him on the back of the head, but Mila laughed. "I think I'll be okay, but I'll keep that in mind."

They walked around the corner and entered the four-story building through the front door, the garage not having an entrance of its own. Mila checked the mail, and then they entered the small elevator, riding it to the top.

"I can't believe Preston Meriwether is a Magical, and he needs *our* help," Mila mused as the elevator passed the second level.

"He's really that big of a deal?"

"Uh, yeah." She gave him an incredulous look. "He's one of the richest men in the world. He has his fingers in basically everything, from internet companies to electric cars. He even just started a company that will be mining asteroids, once the tech catches up. He's big time."

Finn was fairly unimpressed, having come from literal royalty and grown up in a palace that was more precious metal than stone. "So, he's rich? That's it?"

"I mean, that's a big part of it," Mila said, slightly sobered, "but he also runs a number of charities that help people all over the world."

That piqued Finn's interest. "Really? Like what?"

The elevator *dinged*, and the doors opened on their floor. Mila fished her keys from her pocket and headed for the door. "He has a foundation that feeds millions of starving people. Another one is working to save rainforests, and I think he's working with the Gates Foundation to wipe out malaria or something."

Finn nodded, liking what he was hearing. "He sounds like a stand-up guy. Now I'm a little eager to meet him."

Mila laughed, opening the front door. "So that's your thing, eh? Helping people?"

"Yeah," Finn said seriously. "Money is just a means to an end. It's how that means is used that's interesting to me."

"Speaking of…" Mila dropped her keys in the basket on the counter by the door, scooping up Danica's keys from a foot away and putting them in the basket as well. "Don't forget the guy from the bank will be here in an hour and a half to set up the accounts for the mine."

Finn, Penny, and Mila had spent many nights thinking up how best to sell the gold they got from Draupnir. So far, they had been using the Cash for Gold places in Denver and surrounding cities, but they had personally depressed the local market for gold and decided that they needed a new way to offload it.

They had been at a dead-end when Penny found an old gold mine for sale in middle-of-nowhere Idaho. The listing said it had been mined out, but that there was the potential for more if the mine was expanded. The price was right, so they contacted the owner, an old guy living the good life in Coeur d'Alene. He agreed to direct payments, and they signed some paperwork and wired him a hundred grand as a down payment.

Now he and Mila were the owners of a defunct gold mine a thousand miles away that they had never seen. But it was the perfect cover for selling large amounts of gold.

"Sounds like we have time for a shower and a quick lunch," Finn said, opening the fridge and pulling out a package of thick-cut bacon. "How does a BLT sound?"

Mila rolled her eyes back and moaned. "Like heaven. I'm going to shower first if you don't mind."

"Not at all." He pulled a frying pan from the large drawer beside the stove.

Danica opened her bedroom door and stepped out, drying her hair with a damp towel, dressed in her lounging clothes. "Oh, hey, guys. I didn't hear you come in. How did it go?"

Penny, who had fished the box of Charleston Chew Minis from Finn's bomber jacket, looked up and waved before eating another candy. Danica smiled and held out her hand. Penny begrudgingly placed one chew in her hand.

"Thanks, darlin'," the elf said with a wink.

"It went like a hurricane at a wedding," Mila said, peeling off her thick wool sweater, leaving the black Gortex compression shirt. "Luckily, we were ready for a hurricane. How was your day at the hospital?"

Danica put her towel around her neck and flopped onto the couch. "It was crazy. So, get this. A guy who had been attacked by wolves was brought into the emergency room. Fucking *wolves!*"

"Holy shit." Mila's eyebrows shot up her forehead. "That hasn't happened in...well, shit, I can't think of the last time that happened."

"Tell me about it," Danica said, putting her feet up on the coffee table, and crossing her ankles. "Poor guy didn't make it. Died on the table. But here's the weird thing: I went down to check him out, and the wounds were laced with magic. Nothing anyone would have noticed unless they were looking for it, but it was there. I couldn't tell if the bites were done by a magical beast, or if someone had used magic to make the wounds look like they were from a wolf, but it was damn weird. Kinda freaked me out, to tell you the truth."

Finn and Mila shared a look, but it was Penny who spoke up.

"Shiri chi chir squee?"

Danica looked from Penny to Finn for the translation.

"She asked if you know about Preston Meriwether's magical zoo," Finn said, laying the first slices of bacon in the hot pan, the apartment filling with sizzling, and the mouthwatering smell of bacon.

Danica barked a laugh. "You think he has something to do with it? There is no way that guy killed a dude with magical beasts. He's practically a saint in the Magical community. Hell, he's practically a saint in the Peabrain community. I heard he once donated ten million dollars to an orphanage for half-breed Magical children who had been abandoned by their parents. A guy like that doesn't feed people to magical wolves."

Finn had seen a lot of people in his many years of life, some of whom were very rich and loved by the public, as Meriwether seemed to be. He would have to disagree with Danica's blanket statement, but he would reserve judgment on the man until he met him.

Finn made four sandwiches, slicing the tomato nice and thin, and adding salt and pepper, just the way he liked it. Sitting around the coffee table, they crunched their way through the toasted sandwiches. Danica told them about the rest of her day; nothing special, but Finn found it was good to get a day off your chest so you could relax, so he was more than willing to hear about Regina's and Mark's baby, and how the cafeteria had stopped serving Danica's favorite soup.

Mila told the story of Finn fixing the trees, to Danica's open-mouthed amazement, and Finn's protests that it wasn't really all that big a deal. Penny was the one who made it clear that Mila was the one who'd saved most of the elves' lives with her quick work with the healing potions. Danica was so shocked by the whole tale that she didn't even notice when Penny ate the last quarter of her unattended BLT.

After dinner, Mila hit the shower while Finn cleaned up their plates and glasses, then he took his turn washing off the small twigs, brambles, and leaves he had unintentionally collected on their trek through the woods. He toweled off and stepped out of the master bathroom into Mila's bedroom, where he had some things in a small section of her closet.

He appreciated that she had given up what space she had for him, but he knew this was not a long-term solution. He needed to find a place of his own, but he also didn't want to be far from Mila and Danica, the two people he counted most as friends on *Earth* so far.

He selected a pair of bright red boxers, the only thing he wore of any color. His black t-shirt and jeans had been a staple for as long as he had been on his own; plus, it made selecting what to wear on any given day a non-issue.

A man and woman's voice he didn't recognize came filtering through Mila's door from the living room. He tensed and finished fastening his leather holster around his chest before pulling the handle of Fragar out and taking hold of the door handle. In one quick burst, he pulled the door open and leaped out, his eyes scanning for the threat.

Sitting at the dining table beside the kitchen were Mila, and a man and a woman both in suits. All three jumped at his aggressive entrance, the woman and man letting out squeaks of fright.

Mila frowned and rolled her eyes. "Finn, you remember we have a meeting with the bank people?" she asked, indicating the two at the table with open-handed gestures.

Finn went from narrow-eyed aggression to large, toothy smile in a heartbeat, and quickly slipped Fragar back into its holster. He strode across the condo, taking a quick glance around for Penny, and seeing her tucked into a corner of the couch, out of sight, napping while she waited for the strangers to leave. Danica was nowhere to be seen—probably in her room or out for a run.

Finn held out his big hand to the woman first and shook hers before turning to the man and doing the same. "Hello. Sorry about that. We had some intruders a few weeks back, and I completely forgot you were coming while I was in the shower. Finnegan Dragonbender, it's nice to meet you."

The man spoke up first, while the woman blinked in surprise a few times, taking in his huge frame.

"I'm Benjamin Groot, and this is my associate Silva Durant. She will be in charge of your account and your primary contact at the bank. It's very nice to meet you, Mr. Dragonbender. That's an unusual name. Where is it from, if you don't mind me asking?"

Finn smiled and sat down at the table. "It's Canadian, but please, call me 'Finn.' So, how is this going to work?"

Silva finally recovered and cleared her throat, opening a leather binder and sifting through some papers while she spoke. "I have put together some numbers, and the process we need to go through to exchange the gold you withdraw from the mine. Mr. Groot here is our appraiser and will be taking a look at the samples you have brought from your mine. Ms. Winters said you had several bars here we could take a look at?"

Mila stood and made her way around the table. "Yeah, I have them in the safe. I'll grab one."

Mr. Groot opened a large, leather rolling bag that sat on the floor beside his chair—a bag Finn had failed to notice—and removed several rolled-up tool bags. He had set up a little workstation by the time Mila returned, and she placed a large gold bar on the piece of black felt he had laid out on the table in front of him.

He started working, doing his weighing and measuring, while Ms. Durant continued.

"As you know, the bank deals in bullion, so we will be able to take the bars directly and give you spot price minus one percent. How much do you estimate the mine will produce?"

Finn looked up at the ceiling, mumbling as he did the math. "Uh, let's see. Nine bands times four pounds, times sixteen ounces… Thirty days in a month…" He cleared his throat. "About two thousand ounces a month, by my numbers."

She nodded and wrote down the figure. "Okay, that's not too bad for an old mine. That small a deposit should be fine for the downtown branch. If you want to have it shipped directly to me, I can take care of everything for you. I'm just going to need to have the name of the mining company and your paperwork that I sent Ms. Winters last week. And a form of ID."

Finn produced a folded piece of paper that had nothing but a few runes scribbled on it, and she looked it over, filling out the pertinent information her nonmagical eyes saw on the "ID".

An hour later, the two bankers left, Mr. Groot's rolling bag heavy with three gold bars. They had concluded business with a firm handshake and a stack of signed documents. As of now, he and Mila were the proud owners of a very profitable gold mine, and they didn't even have to mine it.

Finn held up the small plastic cards and handed Mila the one with her name on it. "Well, I guess we're rich. This is a lot of money, right?"

She smiled and laughed. "Yeah, nearly three million dollars is a lot. Now don't go spending it all in one place."

"No promises," he said, slipping the card into his back pocket.

CHAPTER FIVE

That evening, Finn made dinner for the whole household, fish with lemon garlic sauce and steamed asparagus. The four friends sat down at the large coffee table and watched the first couple of episodes of *Firefly* for the third time. It was turning out to be Finn's favorite show, and even though he hated to admit it, Captain Mal was even better than the Duke in a lot of ways.

Mila and Danica cleaned up while Finn contemplated the problem of having somewhere to call his own. He didn't want to move out, but he also knew that sleeping on their couch was not a long-term situation.

He was about to ask Penny to get online and find them a place close by when he heard the neighbors' music quietly thumping through the walls. It wasn't obnoxious, but it gave him an idea.

"Hey, Mila." He stood and walked to the safe, entering the code and opening it up. "How much cash do we have?"

Mila looked up from the sink, where she was doing the

dishes, and bit her lip in thought for a few seconds. "I think there's about five hundred thousand or something. Why?"

He squatted down and started counting out the stacks of hundreds they had gotten from cleaning out all the Cash for Gold places around Denver.

"I think it's time I got my own place. You guys don't need me snoring away on your couch. And I just thought of the perfect place to get."

He was facing the safe, so he missed the frown that crossed Mila's and Danica's faces.

They looked at one another, and a '*well, it had to happen eventually*' look passed between them.

Penny hopped off the back of the couch and glided over to land on his shoulder. "Squee, shi chi chi!"

Finn smiled at her and winked. "I know they like us here, but to tell you the truth, my back is starting to hate that couch," he hiked a thumb at the large, L-shaped piece of furniture. "Besides, I think this will work out pretty well."

He closed the safe and turned to see the women wearing sad expressions.

He smiled. "Don't be so dour. I think you'll like this."

He walked to the front door and exited, everyone trailing on his heels.

"Where are you going?" Mila finally asked, drying her hands on a dishtowel she had brought with her.

Instead of answering, he stepped up to their neighbor's front door and loudly knocked.

"Their music isn't all that loud," Danica said, raising her eyebrow.

The door opened to reveal a woman in her mid-twenties. The music was much louder now that the door was open.

"Hello. Sorry, I didn't realize you were home. I can turn down the music." The woman gave them an apologetic smile, slightly intimidated that there were three people on her doorstep, one of whom had a rather intense-looking blue lizard on his shoulder.

"The music is fine," Finn reassured her with a smile of his own. "I was actually wondering if you would be willing to sell your condo to me?"

Everyone but Finn blinked in surprise for a few seconds. The door opened all the way to reveal a man about the same age as the woman, their rings showing that they were married.

He gave everyone a confused look before fixing his eyes on Finn. "Hello. I don't think we've met." He held out a hand. "I'm Simon, and this is my wife Becky. Can we help you guys?"

"I would like to purchase your condo," Finn reiterated, shaking Simon's hand.

Simon laughed until he realized Finn was completely serious.

"I don't think now is a great time to sell," he said uncertainly. "The market is still climbing. We were hoping to sell in a couple of years and build a place out in the mountains, but it just wouldn't be worth it to us right now."

Finn never lost his smile. "How much are you hoping to get for it?"

Simon blew out a long breath while he considered, finally barking a laugh. "Well, we got the place pretty early, so we only have about five in it, but I'm thinking it could be worth a million in a few years, the way the market is going."

Finn glanced at Penny, who knew this game all too well, and she showed teeth in her smile. She was thinking the same as him.

Finn turned back to Simon. "So, if you got a million now, the money would be worth more, since the market is cheaper. And it would go a lot farther now than it would in a few years, right?"

Simon raised an eyebrow. "Yeah…"

"I'll pay you a million right now for the condo, and an extra two hundred thousand if you can move out in the next week."

"*What?*" Mila, Simon, and Becky all said at once.

Penny and Danica just snickered behind their hands; they knew how dwarves did business—if not from experience, then from stories. Always fair, but with deadlines.

"I'm completely serious," Finn assured the young couple. "I'll even give you a cash advance to make the move easier. How does five hundred thousand sound?"

Becky laughed. "Honestly, it sounds a little too good to be true."

"Hold that thought." Finn put up a finger and jogged back into Mila's condo.

A few seconds later, he came back with a paper bag full of hundred-dollar-bill stacks. He handed the bag to Simon, whose face was frozen in shock.

"That's five hundred. We can have the paperwork done tomorrow, and you two will be millionaires." He smiled at them and put his fists on his hips.

"Uh, that's not really how things are done, Finn. You

don't just hand a bunch of cash to someone before you have a contract," Mila said quietly so as not to offend her neighbors, who were staring into the bag of cash.

"It's fine." He waved off her concern. "We know where they live, so it's not like they could steal it from us."

Everyone clammed up and looked at one another nervously.

Penny caught on before Finn and leaned in to whisper in his ear. "Shi shi." She gave him the eye.

Finn turned a little red. "Sorry, that may have come out wrong," he said to Simon and Becky. "I was merely saying that we could trust you. If you want to sell, that is." He raised his eyebrows at the couple.

They looked at one another, then nodded vigorously. "I say we have a deal, Finn."

Finn clapped his hands together. "Great! We'll meet up tomorrow and get the paperwork done. Thanks, guys. Oh, and it was great to meet you both."

The shocked couple backed into their condo, the brown paper bag full of cash held out in front of them as if it might try to bite them, before they slowly closed the door.

Mila turned to Finn and put her hands on her hips. "What the fuck was that?"

Finn shrugged. "That's how rich people get shit done. We don't need all the money, but we do need the space. It was a good deal for everyone."

"I guess so, but they probably think we're drug dealers or something, having that much cash on hand." She shook her head. "Besides, I know it's just next door, but we're going to miss having you two in the house."

Finn smiled as he led the two women back into their

condo. "That's the best part. We can knock down this wall and make one big place. I was thinking we needed not just a place for me and Penny to sleep, but a whole bunch of other things like a dojo and a workbench, not to mention places to store all the gear we're going to be accumulating. Imagine this place twice as big and outfitted the way we need it. Besides, Penny already hid the top floor of the building from the Kashgar, so that's one less thing to worry about."

He saw the look on Mila's and Danica's faces slowly change from sad to ecstatic as they considered the possibilities.

"I'll contact a lawyer and get the paperwork drawn up," Mila said before giving him a big hug, which Danica joined in on. "I love this idea."

CHAPTER SIX

The next morning, Finn and Mila drove south forty minutes out of town to just northwest of Castle Rock. From there, they pulled off Interstate 25 and headed west for a couple of miles, till they came to a large, gated drive. Trees lined the front of the estate, and with the assistance of a ten-foot stone wall, blocked any views of the house and grounds beyond.

Mila pulled to the curb and checked the address once again to be sure.

"This looks like the place. Meriwether knows how to live it up."

Penny huffed a ball of smoke from where she stood on Finn's leg and leaned against the window, taking the place in.

"I agree." Finn nodded, squinting. He translated for Mila. "We're pretty sure there's a concealment spell on the whole property. See how you can't get even a glimpse past the trees? That's by design. I would be willing to bet that the neighbors don't notice this place unless they are looking for the address."

"Is that a guard at the gate?" Mila asked, seeing a small, arched door recessed in the stone wall beside the large, steel gate.

"I would think so. Pull up, and let's find out," he suggested.

She tapped the gas and the Hellcat growled its way into the drive. She came to a stop at the heavy gates that looked like they could stop a tank if they wanted to and rolled down her window.

A man in a black suit stepped out of the darkened arch and, one hand in his coat, leaned forward to greet them.

"Mr. Dragonbender and Ms. Winters. Mr. Meriwether has been expecting you. Please pull up to the main house and park at the front steps."

He disappeared into the shadow of his arch before they could say anything in response, and the gate swung open on silent motors.

"Fancy," Mila commented, putting the car in drive and rumbling up the long, tree-lined drive.

They drove for half a mile before the trees thinned out and they got their first view of the house. It was a huge, sprawling, conglomeration of pointed roof peaks and high arched windows set in stone walls. The drive split, one path leading around to the back of the house, and the other leading to a turnaround in front of the wide marble front steps. Mila drove to the front as she had been instructed and pressed the ignition button, the Hellcat rumbling to sleep.

"Well, this is impressive," she said, leaning down to see past Finn and Penny and out the passenger side window.

"It's nice," Finn said. He wasn't exactly unimpressed but growing up in a literal palace had tainted his expectations of wealth. "Are you ready to meet the man?"

Mila sighed and gave him a smile. "Sure. Let's see how the other side lives, shall we?"

Finn pulled on the door handle and slid out of the muscle car, Penny climbing up onto his shoulder. They waited for Mila to come around the car, as she fiddled with the short, red leather jacket that he liked.

"I feel like I'm underdressed for this," she mused, frowning at her black tights and calf-high, heeled boots.

"We're here for work, not a ball. You look great, magic boots and all."

He held out his arm, and she took it with a chuckle.

"These aren't magic boots."

He made an exaggerated face and leaned back to look at her behind over her shoulder. "Tell that to your ass."

She smacked his arm but blushed slightly at the compliment. "Hey, eyes front, bub."

He chuckled and smiled down at her.

They reached the top step, and Finn reached for the large, metal knocker on the two-story wooden door, but the slab opened before he could touch it.

Mila sucked in a breath as the door swung open and revealed a ten-foot-tall man wearing a black tuxedo jacket and a crisp white shirt underneath. Finn saw her glance down to the furry, naked legs ending in horse hooves, and smiled as he saw her brain catching up with what she was seeing.

The man took a step sideways, revealing the rest of the horse body that made up his lower half. He waved them inside, and in a haughty, slightly British accent, said, "Please, come in. Mister Meriwether is on the back terrace. I'll show you the way."

"You're a centaur!" Mila blurted out.

The middle-aged horseman smiled at her and nodded. "That I am, Peabrain. Would you please follow me?" He turned and walked with deliberate slowness so as to not lose the two bipedal guests.

Finn was impressed. Centaurs prided themselves on their independent natures, and it was extraordinarily rare to see one in a servant's position. Either this Preston fellow was worthy of the centaur's respect and loyalty, or he was some kind of monster. Those were the only circumstances under which Finn had ever seen a centaur work for someone else.

They made their way through the enormous house that was, somehow, modern and traditional at the same time. The art on the walls leaned toward the modern, but there were a few impressionist paintings in the mix that kept the view interesting to his eyes.

The centaur led them to a large set of glass doors and opened one for them. Beyond the glass was a large, marble patio that looked out over beautiful grasslands, offering a view of the Rockies in the distance.

"This way. Mister Meriwether is at the table, having his breakfast."

Finn glanced to the side and saw a large, wooden table with several serving plates containing everything from eggs and bacon to delicately rolled crepes stuffed with fruit. At the head of the table was a giant of a man in a thick, cream-colored sweater and dark blue jeans. He had a thick thatch of black hair, and a set of large, curved horns coming from the sides of his forehead.

As they stepped out onto the veranda, Preston Meriwether turned toward them and smiled, his large, bovine nose curling up slightly.

Finn, for the first time, was shocked. He had never met a minotaur before. They were a very private species and rarely traveled from their homeworld. Nothing he had found about *Earth* said there was a population of them at all.

Preston stood and ate up the distance between them with long strides. He held out his large hand, and Finn took it automatically, the size of his own hand small in comparison.

"Hello, Mr. Dragonbender. It is a real pleasure to meet you. Garret and Hermin can't stop talking about you and your friend, Ms. Winters."

His voice was deep and pleasant, and his eyes warm. He took Mila's hand into his and nearly engulfed half her forearm in his palm. "A pleasure, Ms. Winters." He then glanced up at Penny and offered her a finger to shake. "Ms. Penny. I am sorry, but no one has been able to tell me your surname. But I suppose a faerie dragon should have her secrets." He gave her a wink that made her blush and puff out her chest in an unconscious show of pleasure. "Please, come and join me. I was just having breakfast."

Finn guessed he was used to people not knowing how to take his true form, and was gracious in their shock, leading them to the table, where an elven maid in the traditional black and white dress of the position cheerily placed plates and silverware down for the three new guests. Finn noted her happy demeanor, making a tick in the 'worthy' column of the balance sheet he was keeping in his head about Meriwether.

After a second's thought, Finn made two ticks; one for the happy maid, and one for the way Preston had handled their shock at seeing him.

Finn sat across the table from Mila and Penny. Penny was genuinely surprised when the maid provided a thin purple, embroidered cushion for her. They all settled in as a second maid came and filled their cups with coffee and orange juice.

"Please, fill your plates," Meriwether encouraged, taking a sip of his coffee, but waiting to eat until they all had food.

Penny, not one to be shy, began working the large serving spoon in the scrambled eggs like a pro, even going so far as to drop a scoop on both Finn's and Mila's plates as they slowly began making their choices. Soon, everyone had a good, hearty breakfast piled onto the thin porcelain plates, but no one had more than Penny, who had taken the open invitation to heart.

Finn chuckled when two of the five sausages she had taken fell off her overcrowded plate. She quickly stuffed them in her mouth as if nothing had happened.

Once everyone else was eating, Meriwether dug in, not showing any reservations about doing so in front of guests. He was a large man, making Finn look normal sized in comparison, and he evidently needed to eat to maintain that size. In the span of twenty minutes, he ate four plates full and didn't seem overstuffed in the least.

"This is wonderful, Mr. Meriwether," Mila said, wiping at the corner of her mouth with her napkin. "I have to say, I'm a big fan of the charities you organize. I appreciate that there is someone out there with the wealth that you have, who genuinely cares about people."

He waved the comment off. "I don't do anything that most people don't want to do. I have the means, and I enjoy solving problems, Ms. Winters. It's nothing more."

"I don't know, Mr. Meriwether," Mila pressed. "There are a lot of very wealthy people out there who don't seem to care about much more than the number in their account."

"First, please call me 'Preston.' 'Mr. Meriwether' makes me sound like a Bond villain." He chuckled along with the rest of them. "And secondly, you're right that there are a lot of people who only look to raise their status with their wealth, but there are just as many that work quietly in the background to make the world better. Just remember that the news you hear is for-profit nowadays. The world isn't nearly as bad as you've been told. I don't think what I'm choosing to do with my money is anything special, just a product of my upbringing."

He gave them a toothy smile. "My mother would twist my horns off if she thought I was being anything but generous. My altruism comes from fear, God rest her soul." He folded his hands, resting his elbows on the table and his chin on his fingers. "Ask your friend here," he nodded toward Finn. "He is a prince after all if those magical tattoos are real. He grew up with more money than there is on Earth, but here he sits, ready to help a schlub like me."

Mila gave Finn a look he didn't like all that much. It was

an expression that he had come to dread in his exile, one worn by someone when they realized how much influence his name actually had.

He decided he needed to keep that look off her face at all costs. She was far too special to him to think of him as anything but the guy she'd saved at a Kum & Go on a random night.

"I haven't been a royal for a long time…not the way you think of them, anyway." Finn shifted in his chair and looked Preston in the eye. "What can the ladies and I do for you, Preston?"

Preston saw that he had hit a bit of a nerve with the dwarf, and wisely pressed ahead before Mila got caught up in it too much. He stood and waved for them to follow. "Come. I need to show you a few things before we get to the heart of it."

Penny glanced from Mila to Finn and chose to ride on Mila's shoulder, her presence distracting the woman while Finn frowned, his mood soured with the reminder of his family.

He made a mark in the *'monster'* column in his mind.

CHAPTER SEVEN

Preston led them down the veranda to a path that wound its way through an ornate garden of exotic flora. Some of the signs warned passersby to not step off the path due to carnivorous plants. The walk was filled with pleasant talk between Preston and Mila, with Finn following a few paces behind, trying to figure the billionaire out.

He seemed genuine, and the comment about Finn's past life had been dropped without much prompting, but still, Finn had a suspicion that there might be more to this man than the public image he portrayed.

Penny kept looking back to check on him, and he waved off her concern with a half-smile. She had seen him in his contemplative moods enough times to know not to bother him and turned back to listen in on whatever Preston was saying.

Fishing his box of Charleston Chews out of his jacket pocket, Finn ate a few, out of habit more than anything, and considered why he would help this guy. Money was not an issue, especially now that they had the mine up and running. But he needed favors. The expensive kind.

Over the last few weeks on *Earth*, Finn had realized that while the machine herself was running acceptably well, thanks in most part to the Elemental that the Huldu wouldn't stop talking about, there were other threats to this great ship. And if treasure hunting had taught Finn anything, it was that the truly precious treasures needed protecting.

The *Earth* was riddled with wars and famine and all sorts of disasters, but the Peabrains had those under control, for the most part. And the magical phenomena that threatened to spill out into society was being taken care of by the Huldu and a few other notable entities. Seeing his place in the mess had taken him a few nights of hard thinking, but once it hit him, he felt like an idiot for not seeing it from the start.

On the original voyage, a large number of dwarves had booked passage, his distant cousin Fafnir among them. Most of the dwarves were weapon and artifact smiths, and they had brought almost all of their items with them; that was the original bit of knowledge that had turned Finn on to finding *Earth* in the first place. Now that the dwarves were all gone, there was no one left who truly understood the power of those artifacts, as was plainly evident the day before, when the elves had nearly destroyed an entire forest by a mere miscalculation.

The *Earth* needed someone like him to police the artifacts before those trying to use them got out of hand and did some real damage. To tell the truth, he was surprised the ship had lasted this long without a dwarf aboard. Now that he was here permanently, he understood it was where he could do the most good. And for that, he would need allies. And lots of favors.

"Here we are," Preston said in his pleasant baritone as the path came to an end at a vine-covered brick wall. He swiped an electronic pad with his finger, and a metal door set into the brick unlocked with a *ka-chunk* and swung open.

When they stepped through, Finn was confused at first, thinking the brick was the wall of a long, low building, but he soon saw that it was, in fact, the perimeter wall of a large zoo. The path they were on was obviously a private entrance for Preston, but it quickly led out onto one of the main paths, and by an open-air enclosure that held several blue, glowing beetles, larger than a Great Dane. Dozens of people walked the path, stopping at the exhibit, including several children, who jumped and pointed at the lazy beetles sunning themselves on the rocks.

"Welcome to the Menagerie," Preston said with a bovine smile that seemed more human than Finn thought could come from a bull's lips.

They stepped off the private path and onto the public thoroughfare, several of the visitors smiling and waving to Preston, who returned every greeting in kind.

Mila sucked in a breath, looking at the beetles, and Finn glanced that way. All three of the hulking bugs had stood up on their rocks and were obviously staring at them. The one closest to the path raised its front leg and began to wave.

It was such an odd display that the people gathered

around the enclosure's edge began to look over their shoulders.

Mila shyly raised a hand and waved at the shiny blue beetle, who then took a slight bow before settling back down on its rock as if nothing out of the ordinary had happened.

The people, however, were buzzing with excitement at the odd show.

"I must say, Ms. Winters," Preston said, giving her an appraising look before motioning for them to continue, "the scarabs have not been that active in a long, long time. They are rather picky about who they interact with. You must be someone special indeed."

Mila reddened as they made their way past several more displays. " Insects and I have always had an…understanding."

Preston gave her a sideways, appraising look. "Interesting."

They continued on, winding through what Finn was sure was a top-notch zoo. It rivaled anything he had seen on his journeys, making the one at his father's capital look sterile and cruel in comparison. The enclosures mimicked the creatures' natural habitat and gave them plenty of room to move around while keeping the observers and creatures all perfectly safe. Each of the enclosures was open to the air, but when Finn saw a particularly aggressive young roc try to fly out of its enclosure, the bluish glow of a magical barrier turned the large bird back. It was quite the show of power, to enclose zoo exhibits with magic.

Eventually, they made their way across the grounds,

and Preston led them to another gate labeled Employees Only. He once again used his fingerprint to open the door, and led them into a building, raucous with barking and growling dogs.

The interior was made of cinderblocks, painted with shiny gray paint that gave the place a clinical look. There were several chain-link fences with gates that served as pens between cinder block walls. As they passed by, Finn was surprised to see that the dogs were not dogs at all—at least, not in the traditional sense. They were hellhounds.

The hounds stood nearly five-foot at the shoulder and had long, wide snouts full of glistening, silver teeth. Their coats were a motley of colors, from a drab brown to white and black, and every spotted combination between. Finn had seen hellhounds before, but these were a little smaller than ones found in the wild, and resembled a cross between a border collie and a Great Dane, with short body hair, and long hair on the tail and legs. All in all, they were very pretty dogs; except for the glowing red eyes. Those were a little disconcerting.

"Hello, Anita." Preston had to nearly shout to be heard over the constant barking.

A slender black-haired elf in a long, white lab coat nearly jumped out of her skin as she spun from the computer she had been working at on the counter.

"Sorry, I didn't mean to frighten you," he continued loudly. "This is Finnegan Dragonbender and his associate Dr. Mila Winters, along with Penny. They're the ones I told you about the other day."

Anita motioned for them to follow her, and she led them out the back door to a yard that was obviously used to let the hounds get some exercise, if the ripped-up turf and various half-destroyed toys were any indication. As soon as the party was outside, the hounds quit their barking, and Anita pulled earplugs out of her ears and dropped them into her pocket. She pulled a pack of cigarettes from the other pocket and lit one with a flame from the end of her finger.

"Sorry about that," she said, nervously pushing a pair of wire-framed glasses up her nose and taking a quick pull on the cigarette. "The hounds did not imprint on me, so they tend to be a little rambunctious. Makes talking around them nearly impossible. Oh my god. Is that a faerie dragon? You have to let me examine it. I didn't think there were any left! Where did you get it?"

Her ability to talk, smoke, and change subjects all in one breath made it hard for Finn to follow, but when she reached out to pick up Penny, he finally caught up.

However, it was Mila who took a step back, keeping Penny out of Anita's reach.

"I wouldn't do that if I were you," Mila said with care. "Not if you want to keep all your fingers and your skin. Penny doesn't like to be picked up."

Penny puffed a yellow flame and narrowed her eyes at the black-haired elf.

Anita stopped in her tracks, a look of embarrassment crossing her face. "Sorry. I didn't mean any offense. I've just never seen a live specimen before. I've only read about them in Herchal's journals."

"Shir chchchi!" Penny shot another gout of flame to punctuate the point.

"She says she's not a specimen," Finn translated.

Anita looked from Finn to Penny and back. "They can talk? I thought they were just a smaller version of wyverns? Intelligent, but no more than, say, a dog or horse."

Finn laughed. "Penny is probably the smartest person here, by a long shot." He cleared his throat and glanced over to Preston. "Can we move this along? I'm sure your time is precious, as is ours."

"Yes," Preston agreed, "my apologies. I have a bit of a problem. One of the hellhounds has been stolen, and I need to have it recovered as soon as possible."

Finn blinked in confusion. "I'm sorry, no disrespect intended, but that's not really what we do. We find *artifacts*, particularly dwarven ones. I'm sure there are plenty of qualified people who can find your hound for you."

"Unfortunately," Anita chimed in, her fascination with Penny abated for the moment, "we tried that already, and they didn't have any success. The problem is that the hound in question was pregnant, and by now, her pups are already grown. Tracking spells don't work on hellhounds, and once they've imprinted on a person, they won't respond to anyone but their master, so magical whistles and such don't work either."

Finn frowned and glanced at Penny, who gave him a shrug. Mila gave a shrug too.

"Yeah, I understand how hellhounds work." Finn cocked his head as he thought about that further, and added, "Sort of. I've come across a few in my travels, but I still don't understand why you think I can help."

"Because the hound was taken just after she was impregnated," Anita said as if it were obvious.

Finn was starting to get a little frustrated with the woman, but Preston stepped in to clarify.

"When hellhounds breed, they tend to be a little boisterous, to the point that the females don't always survive. Since there are so few of the magnificent creatures left, we take every precaution to ensure the female's survival. A few years back, I purchased a dwarven-made ring of stone skin. We use it to make the female much more resilient during mating and the resulting pregnancy. This particular female was stolen while still wearing the ring."

"Ah," Finn said, finally getting where this was all going. "So you want me to find the ring, and hope that the hound is still attached to it, is that it?"

"Precisely." Preston smiled. "The problem is that the hound would have had her pups nearly a month ago, and as you may or may not know, hellhounds grow very fast. The pups will be fully matured by now and could be a threat to a lot of people. If the pups imprinted on the thief at birth, then that person will have an entire pack at his disposal."

Mila raised an eyebrow. "How many pups are in one litter? You make it sound like a ton."

"Anywhere from twenty to thirty," Anita said before sucking one last, long drag from her cigarette, and dropping what was left into a bucket full of butts.

"Twenty to thirty?" Mila balked. "That's insane."

"There's another problem," Finn said with a sigh. "If the ring was still on the hound when she gave birth, then its magic would have transferred to the pups. This transference was one of the problems found with skin transformation talismans. It's one reason they are so hard to come by."

Mila put two and two together. "So, you're telling us there is a pack of twenty to thirty hellhounds out there, under some thief's control, with stone skin? That sounds like a fucking nightmare."

Preston and Anita shared a worried look.

"Actually," Preston admitted, "We didn't know that the ring's properties would transfer. This is, perhaps, a little worse than we thought."

Finn grunted his agreement, pulling out his box of Chews and tossing a few in his mouth. After he finally swallowed, he frowned.

"Okay, we'll take the case."

CHAPTER EIGHT

After Finn and Mila agreed to help Preston Meriwether track down his missing hellhound, they began negotiations for compensation.

Mila was shocked at the extravagant numbers Preston was throwing their way, but Finn waved off the offer.

"We don't need money, to be honest."

Preston's eyebrows went up. "If not money, what were you thinking of as compensation?"

Finn glanced at Penny, riding Mila's shoulder. The faerie dragon grinned, knowing what he was thinking.

"A favor," he said firmly. "It's my favorite currency on a new world, and I think we're going to need a few in the future."

"I don't know." Preston crossed his thick arms and frowned. "An open-ended favor can be very dangerous for someone in my position. I have a public image to uphold, for the good of the magical community."

Finn liked where Preston's head was; personally, he

wouldn't give an open favor as payment for anything, unless he trusted the person completely.

"That's a fair stance. How about we put some limitations on it, then?"

"I'm listening."

Finn decided he could work with someone who was willing to listen.

"We will only call in the favor if it helps the community as a whole. No personal shit, just community-based favors."

A smile spread across Preston's bovine lips, and he held out a hand. "Deal. I like the way you think, dwarf. It seems the stories about your people are unfounded."

Finn chuckled and shook the minotaur's hand. "I wouldn't say they're unfounded. Most of the dwarves I know are right bastards. I left that life for a reason."

Anita seemed like she wanted to get back to work, but was too nervous to say so, but Preston picked up on her jitters and gave her an out with a smile.

"Anita, I think we're done here. I'll be giving Mr. Dragonbender your number so they can reach out if they have any questions later."

She brushed a strand of black hair behind her ear and opened the door, filling the exercise yard with barking and howling from inside. "That's fine. I don't sleep much, so feel free to call anytime." She fished the earplugs from her lab coat's pockets and slipped them into her ears before closing the door behind her, cutting off the racket of hellhounds.

"Come with me," Preston said, leading them to a side gate. "Kal, my butler, has some parting gifts for you: a video from the surveillance system at the Menagerie, and what notes we have on the stone skin ring. It's not much, but it's all we have, unfortunately."

They stepped out onto the public path and wound their way back toward Preston's private entrance.

"So, this all happened two months ago?" Mila asked, glancing up at Preston, her brow furrowed.

"That's right." Preston held out a hand, directing her to take the next turn.

"Who did you hire to look for the hound first? What kind of resources did they have at their disposal?" Mila raised an eyebrow.

Finn fished out his box of Charleston Chews and shook a few into his hand while he tried to figure out what Mila was getting at.

Penny heard the candies shaking and leaped from Mila's shoulder to his in one bound, making Mila stumble slightly.

"Chishi," Penny said with an embarrassed smile at Mila, when the small woman glanced back in surprise at the sudden move.

"She says 'sorry,'" Finn said and held out the box to Mila, who shook her head.

Penny held out her hand, not wanting the box to be put away before she'd had her fill. Finn gave her a few of the small, chocolate nougat chews before slipping the box back into the pocket of his bomber jacket.

"To answer your question," Preston said, leading them down the side path and swiping his finger over the scanner in the brick wall. "We contacted the Huldu for help and a few of the detectives that are in the know when it comes to us Magicals. I also hired a private investigator, but all those resources came up empty. The video doesn't reveal any kind of distinguishing features we could use to track down the thief, and there's been no criminal activity pointing to the hound, or to the use of the stone skin ring."

Finn nodded as Preston led them back into his gardens and toward the large manor. "That's the problem with criminals. Most of them don't get caught committing the initial crime; it's what they do with the goods that gets them caught."

Preston smiled. "That is what my private investigator told me. The trail went cold, as he put it."

"I have to say," Mila said, putting her hands in the pockets of her jacket against a cold breeze that had suddenly sprung up. "Contacting Finn to find the artifact was a pretty clever move."

"Well," Preston cleared his throat a little and showed her a white smile. "I didn't get rich by looking at opportunities from only one angle. You three are making quite the noise in your own way. Once I heard there was a real dwarf in town, I knew I had to get in contact."

They walked up the half dozen marble steps to the back veranda, and Preston held out his large hand to Finn. "I'm afraid this is where we must part ways. Duty calls in the office."

He and Finn shook hands, and Preston turned to Mila, taking her hand in his a little more gently, and patting it with his free hand in a familiar way.

"Dr. Winters, it has been a pleasure. And Ms. Penny, I hope you never lose that glow; it is far too enchanting."

Penny blushed again and waved off the compliment, her eyes shining with pleasure.

Preston gave them all a half-bow before heading through a side entrance to the house.

Finn and Mila were lost for a second, not sure where to go, when the double glass doors they had originally exited the house from opened, and Kal, the centaur butler, greeted them.

"I understand that you shall be working for Mister Meriwether until this unfortunate event is solved." He gave them a half-bow and motioned for them to enter the house.

"I don't know about working *for,* but we will be working *with* him, yes," Finn clarified, not liking the centaur's tone for some reason. "He said you had some things for us."

Kal gave Finn a forced smile but pulled a flash drive and a manila envelope from inside his black tuxedo jacket and handed them over.

"This is a file with all the surveillance from the night in question. In the envelope, you will find the original notes that came with the ring. Hopefully, something in there can be of help." From his front pocket, he pulled out a thick business card and handed that over as well. "Mister Meriwether told me to give you his personal number, along with our zoologist Anita's as well. Please keep calls to Mister Meriwether to a minimum. He is a very busy man."

Finn gave him a salute with the card before putting it in his back pocket. "Thanks, Kal."

The butler responded with a slight bow, before holding

out a hand to show them the way out. "This way, if you please."

He led them to the front door and opened it for them, standing to the side so they could pass by. Mila walked out, followed by Finn and Penny.

As soon as they were out the door, Kal closed it, almost clipping Finn's heel.

"He seems like a pleasant fellow," Finn said, his eyebrow raised at the large, wooden door.

"Shiri chi chi." Penny shot a small flame at the door for emphasis.

Finn laughed, and Mila cocked her head.

"I think I get her point, but what exactly did she say?"

Finn glanced at Penny, who blushed purple with embarrassment.

"Uh, it was nothing. Just a colloquial insult from her people. She called him a rainbow turd."

Mila furrowed her brow. "A rainbow turd?" A laugh burst out of her. "How is that an insult?"

Finn chuckled with her as they walked down the steps and toward the Hellcat. "It's a bit more intense where she's from."

"Squee shir, shee," Penny said with a huff.

Finn laughed again. "She said it's a bit like calling someone 'fuckface,' but I would say it's more like calling someone a doodoo-head."

Penny folded her arms and glared at him, making Mila laugh.

They climbed into the car, and Mila turned it around using the large roundabout in front of the steps and headed back down the long drive.

"Well, what did you think of Preston?" Finn asked when they had gotten back on the highway.

Mila had been in a bit of a trance since driving out through the gates of the manor, but she snapped out of it with a shake of her head.

"Oh, uh, it was nice."

She flipped on her turn signal and gunned it past a minivan.

"You don't seem all that excited, considering you just met one of the most prominent men on your planet. You seemed overjoyed on the way there," Finn probed, seeing the thoughtful look on her face.

"Huh? Oh, yeah. It was great. I just didn't think he was going to turn out to be a minotaur."

Finn fished out the box of Chews. "Yeah, I didn't really see that one coming, either. I hear their kind are quite the magic users, in addition to being physically superior to almost everyone. It makes sense that he would have become a powerful figure in the nonmagical world."

He saw that she wasn't really listening to him, her head nodding along to some inner dialogue.

"What's wrong with you?"

She glanced at him, then laughed. "Sorry. I was just wondering how Kal works."

Finn squinted, trying to figure out what she meant. "I suppose he has time off, like he would at a regular job."

"No, I mean how he works physically. Like, does he have two rib cages? And if so, does that mean he has two hearts? Two digestive systems? Does the first system just dump into his second stomach? It doesn't make sense." Her eyes were wide and a little frantic.

Finn and Penny exchanged a worried look.

"Well," Finn began. "From what I understand, his heart and lungs are in the human torso, and the rest is in the horse torso."

She thought about that for a few seconds before shaking her head. "That would mean that his throat goes all the way through the human part of his body. You could punch him in the gut, and effectively choke him out."

Finn chuckled. "You just met a centaur *and* a minotaur, and the thing that is hanging you up is how long Kal's throat is?"

She laughed. "I suppose that is a little crazy, isn't it?"

"No crazier than the fact that we're doing eighty miles an hour by burning a refined liquid in a metal block. The universe is a weird place; don't let it get to you."

She smiled at him, then stomped on the accelerator, launching them down the freeway. "I'm hungry. That breakfast was good, but I was too nervous to eat much. I'm thinking Reubens for lunch."

"I don't know what that is, but it sounds good to me."

"Chi, chi!"

CHAPTER NINE

The elevator opened on the top floor of the condo, and Simon and Becky were waiting for Finn and Mila in the hallway.

"Hey, guys." Becky was extra chipper, nearly bouncing. "We found a place online last night, took a look this morning, and we're ready to move on it. When will the bank guy be here to sign papers? We're so excited! I can't believe this is all real. Will there be time for us to get some food? Maybe a shower? I just can't believe our luck!"

Finn was a little taken aback by the verbal assault from the nearly vibrating woman. He looked over to Mila, who was just as shocked by Becky's manic eyes.

They both stood in silence, trying to think of an answer, till the elevator door *ding*ed and started to close in front of them.

Becky's hand shot into the gap, opening the door again. Her smile was intense.

"Uh, the title guy said he would be here in about an

hour," Mila said, finally finding her voice. "Is that an okay time for you?"

Simon, seeing his wife's runaway exuberance turning the hallway into a creep show, pulled her back from the door to let Finn and Mila out.

They stepped off as Becky seemed to realize she was becoming a little too intense and calmed down a bit, but her eyes still sparkled like a little girl's might as she stared into a window display at Christmastime.

The sound of quiet chuckling from Penny made Finn reach back to where she rested in her hammock on his back and flick her. She quieted, and Simon raised an eyebrow at him.

"Sorry," he said without explanation.

"Why don't I come get you when the bank's people get here, and we can button this whole thing up this afternoon?" Mila smiled, pulling her key out and unlocking her door.

"That sounds great," Simon said, pulling Becky back toward their door. "We'll see you then."

Finn and Mila waited until the excited couple closed their door, then looked at one another before bursting into laughter.

"Holy shit, that woman was intense," Mila said, opening their door all the way and walking in.

Finn followed close behind. "She knows what she wants. You have to admire that."

"True. That's more than most people have." Mila hung her jacket on a hook by the door and dropped her keys in the basket on the counter. "I'll make the Reubens. Why don't you check out that surveillance video? My laptop is connected to the TV; you can just play it on there."

Finn pulled out the flash drive from his pocket and raised an eyebrow, not exactly sure what to do with it. Penny climbed up from her hammock and rolled her eyes. She scurried down his arm, snatched the small stick, and leaped from his wrist, gliding over to the coffee table to insert the drive into the USB slot.

"Thanks," Finn said, taking off his bomber jacket and hanging it beside Mila's coat before walking to the fridge and grabbing a beer. "Want one?" He held a bottle out to her.

"Sure, but I'll take one of the wheat ones." She reached around him and pulled out two packages from the deli drawer, one of corned beef, and another of swiss cheese.

He popped the bottlecaps and handed the wheat ale to Mila before taking a seat on the couch. Just as his ass hit the cushion, Penny got the video up and playing.

The footage was compiled from several angles, thankfully cut into one long shot that followed a figure through the Menagerie. The video quality was good for a closed-circuit surveillance system, but it was still grainy and tinged green from the night vision.

The figure was obviously a man, wearing a black hoodie and pants. The hood was pulled up, and he wore a ballcap under it, making it even harder to get a good view of him. When he reached to open a door, Finn could see that he was Caucasian, from the skin on his hand, but there were no distinguishing marks on what skin he could see.

Something that hit Finn as odd was the fact that the

thief walked in an upright, confident manner, and not at all like someone who was trying to be sneaky.

He watched as the intruder walked from the parking lot to the front gate. The man spent a few seconds at the gate and apparently picked the lock because it swung open on silent hinges. He then strolled through the park as if he was just there to see the sights. He made a circuitous route, stopping a few times at various pens. He seemed at first like he was taking his time, but Finn noticed he would periodically look at his watch, then leave his current spot abruptly.

"Is he timing his route?" Mila asked from the kitchen, where she was putting sauerkraut and thousand island dressing into a bowl and mixing them together.

"I was just thinking that." Finn looked over his shoulder and gave her a smile. "Good catch."

The door to Danica's room opened, and she stepped out wearing blue pajamas with little rubber ducks printed all over them. She was rubbing the sleep from her eyes, and her hair was fluffed out on one side where she had slept on it.

"Hey, guys." She yawned hugely, hiding her gaping mouth with the back of one hand.

"Good morning, sleepyhead," Mila laughed. "Want a sandwich?"

Danica stumbled her way into the kitchen and squinted down at the sandwich makings, staring at them as her brain caught up with what she was looking at.

After about ninety seconds, she nodded abruptly. "Yeah."

Mila laughed again. "Okay, go sit on the couch, and I'll bring them over when they're done."

Danica zombie-walked to the couch and plopped down beside Finn, putting her feet up on the coffee table. Penny hopped from the table to her lap, sitting up tall, and watching the security footage while patting Danica's leg affectionately. Danica smiled and yawned again, leaning her head on Finn's shoulder.

The man in the video continued to make his way through the various paths until he came to the kennels they had been in earlier that day. He went around the building to the back gate and again picked the lock in a few seconds. When he stepped into the hellhounds' exercise yard, he had a small hitch to his step, but it was only evident when he pivoted to his right.

Finn found it odd that at no time did the thief even accidentally glance in the direction of any of the dozens of cameras he passed. It was as if he knew where each and every one of them was.

"This show sucks," Danica said, combing her fingers through her blonde hair. "Is it some kind of documentary or something?"

Finn chuckled and awkwardly reached over to pat her head where it rested on his shoulder. "It's not a show. It's surveillance footage of a thief stealing a hellhound form Preston Meriwether's Menagerie."

That made Danica sit up.

She turned to him with wide eyes. "You guys are doing a job for Preston Meriwether? Holy shit! Was he as handsome as he is in his photos?"

"If you're into bulls, he is," Mila joked, putting the first two Reubens in the skillet. The sizzle of buttered rye filled the condo.

"Oh yeah. That's so cool. I forget he's a minotaur. His press photos are always done so well, and the concealment spell he uses doesn't leave even a trace of his true form." Danica smiled.

She leaned back into the couch with a renewed interest in the video.

The man opened the back door to the hellhound facility, and the footage cut to a view from an interior camera, showing him entering. He went to a small wall cabinet beside the garage door that led to the loading bay attached to the facility and pulled out a set of car keys. He then opened the garage door, hopped down the two-foot drop to the bay itself, and headed out toward the small parking lot.

When the man landed in the loading bay, Finn noticed him twist slightly, taking most of the drop on his left leg.

"That's interesting," Danica mused, flipping her bottom lip over and over with a long finger as she considered what she was seeing. "He has an injury on his right leg—probably in the thigh, from the way he doesn't put a lot of flex into it."

"Is that going to help us?" Finn asked. "This was two months ago, it would be healed by now. I don't see how that could lead us to him."

"Well..." The elf scooted up on the couch, making Penny lose her balance and hop to the cushion beside Danica. "Sorry." She smiled at Penny before continuing her explanation. "He's walking on it like it's an old injury. See how when he walks normally, you can't see a limp, but he is moving stiffer than a normal person? That tells me he's been living with the injury for a long time. It's probably an old wound that never healed quite right."

Finn nodded. Now that she pointed it out, the man did move like he was used to the inconvenience.

"That's at least something to go on," he agreed.

The man walked up to a large box truck and used the key to get in and start it up. He backed the truck up to the loading ramp and climbed back inside the facility. He rolled a large cage, nearly six feet to a side, up to one of the pens, and then lifted the gate so that the opening of the rolling cage and the pen were lined up. He then, in an almost comical act, pulled a raw steak from the pocket of his hoodie and dropped it into the rolling cage.

The large hellhound sauntered into view. She was magnificent, even in the low quality of the video. She stood taller than the hounds they had seen earlier that day, and her black fur was almost shiny in the halogen lights.

Then it hit Finn that it wasn't her fur that was reflecting the light, but the stone that covered her. It looked like obsidian, but in finer detail than any statue could obtain. Each hair of her fur was clearly defined, but obviously stiff. It was almost more than the eye could take —living stone that moved with the grace of the large beast.

Mila came in and put down two plates, a sandwich on each, then returned to the kitchen and grabbed two more before settling on Finn's other side.

"Dig in while they're still hot," she said, lifting her sandwich and taking a crunching bite.

They all started eating and watched the end of the video in silence.

Once the hound was in the cage, the man dropped the gate and rolled the cage onto the truck. He took a few minutes strapping it down, then pulled the door closed on the box truck, went around to the front, and drove away. The cameras followed the truck to the back gate, where he once again got out and picked the lock, rolling the chain-link gate open before driving out of camera view. The video stopped, and the screen went black.

They sat in silence while they finished their lunch, each one of them thinking about what they had seen.

Finn was the first one done, and leaned back on the couch, taking a sip of his IPA. "Well, I don't really see how this helps us much. Hopefully, the notes on the ring will get us a scent." He pulled out the manila envelope from where he had folded it up in his back pocket and squeezed the metal pins up that held the flap down and slid the notes out.

"Actually, I think I know that guy," Danica said, wiping thousand-island dressing from her mouth with a paper towel, and setting her sandwich down.

Finn, Mila, and Penny all looked at her in surprise.

Mila was the first to speak. "How can you tell who it is? He never shows his face."

"Well…" She cleared her throat and took a swig of Mila's beer to wash down the rest of her sandwich. "I guess 'know him' is the wrong term. I think I've seen him."

"Who is he?" Finn asked.

"I think he's the guy I told you about who died after he was attacked by wolves. Remember that the wounds were infused with magic? I thought it was someone trying to cover up something else, but hellhounds have about the same jaw pattern as a wolf, and they're already magical. When something strange happens, most of the doctors in the hospital will stop by and take a look. Don't ask, it's a doctor thing. But I saw that the guy who had been mauled had a long scar on his right thigh, probably an old wound, like the guy in the video seems to be suffering from, and he was the same build. What are the chances that a guy with a bad leg steals a hellhound, then a guy ends up killed by some kind of magical dog, and has an old wound on his right leg?"

"Holy shit. Danica, you're a lifesaver. Can we get in to see this guy?"

Finn was all smiles. The chances that one of the only people in the city who could put two and two together happened to be one of his few friends was just another sign that fate had put him here on *Earth* with Mila for a reason.

At least, he liked to think so.

"Sure. Phil is a good guy," Danica said. When she saw the confused looks on their faces, she added, "Phil is the guy in charge of the morgue. I can give him a call."

She got up and went to her room to get her phone, and the doorbell rang. Mila left her place on the couch to answer the door.

"Things are looking up, Penny. Maybe we can find this hound today." Finn smiled and took another sip of his beer.

"Squeek sheir, chi chi." She gave him a half-smile.

"Well, yeah. Obviously, the hounds killed him, but I think we can take care of a few hounds. Besides, it's not like *we* need to deal with them. We can just call Anita and have her come and pick them up. Shit, we might have this thing wrapped up in time to get to karaoke at the Refinery."

Penny gave him a knowing ' famous last words' look but didn't say anything.

"The bank guys are here to sign the paperwork for the condo," Mila said, leading three people in business attire into the living room. "I'll go get Simon and Becky."

She walked out the door, leaving Finn and Penny staring at the small professional team, who stared back at the giant of a man and his pet lizard, lounging on the couch.

After a second, Finn held up his beer.

"You guys want one?"

CHAPTER TEN

The signing of paperwork and transferring of money took a couple of hours, but at the end of it, Finn was the owner of a new condo. Simon and Becky told them they would have movers over the next day to clear the place out, and then everyone shook hands.

Becky was beside herself but held it together until the door closed behind her and Simon. Finn and Mila laughed when they could hear her screams of joy in the hall.

Penny spent the rest of the day going over information on the ring and found what its particular magical "smell" was. She made notes for Finn on a small scrap of paper, her draconic runes completely illegible to anyone but Finn and herself.

As the dragon worked, Mila took a shower and a nap, while Finn excused himself to run an errand.

A week or so ago, he had given a favor to Mila for her help in finding the Helm of Awe. The favor was a little, black, metal card that bound him to her for one favor of her choosing. It could be anything, and he would be magically compelled to do whatever it was she asked.

An open favor like that was not something he gave away lightly; in fact, he had never given one to anyone in his entire life, but he trusted her to use it properly.

However, he felt that the favor was not enough to compensate her for all she had done for him since his arrival, and he liked to give gifts, so he was making his way to the market below Denver's streets, headed to a leather-worker he'd found who made superior quality gear. Once there, he placed an order.

When he returned home a little after eight PM, he found Danica and Mila dressed to go out. Penny was sitting on Mila's shoulder.

"Ready?" Mila asked.

"For what?" Finn frowned.

Danica came to the rescue. "Remember Phil, the guy at the morgue? He said we could come down now, but to hurry because the body will be moved to a funeral home tonight."

"Let's go, then." Finn opened the door he had just come through.

They took Danica's Forester so no one would have to climb into the back seat of the Hellcat; Danica said that she knew the way better anyhow.

At the hospital, she pulled into the employee parking lot close to the back of the main building, and let them in, using her badge on the security door. She led them down a couple of flights of stairs to a yellow and white tiled hall that smelled of bleach and…something else.

A set of double swinging doors with the word '*Morgue*' painted in neat, white letters hung at the end of the hall.

"Okay, Phil is a little odd," Danica warned vaguely before pushing her way through the doors.

Penny scurried down from Finn's shoulder, climbing into her hammock attached to his weapons harness, and gave him a poke when she was ready.

The room beyond looked exactly like every morgue Finn had seen in a movie. Subway-style tiles in an off white, with three stainless steel tables in the center of the room, surrounded by racks of power tools best left to the imagination. The far wall was covered with about twenty small, stainless steel numbered doors, sealed with big latches of the kind that might be found on a walk-in freezer door. To the right was a half-wall with a window that went the rest of the way to the ceiling, enclosing an office.

Sitting at the desk in the office was a tall, thin man in a white lab coat. He had about two days' worth of scruff on his chin and wore thick, black, horn-rimmed glasses, framed by shaggy, black hair that hung down around his neck. His hair was at that odd length that wasn't long but wasn't short either and looked unkempt. He was squinting down at his computer screen, moving the mouse in an erratic pattern, clicking the button like crazy.

Danica led them through the side door of the office just as Phil shouted, "I'm going to rip your kidney out and stitch it to your forehead, you piece of shit!"

"Not even a hello first?" Danica crooned, striking a pose that showed off her figure just a little.

Phil screamed like a little boy going through puberty,

his voice cracking as he jumped up from the computer, brandishing the keyboard like a club. After a few panicked breaths, his shoulders slumped, and he dropped the keyboard on the desk, pressing a palm to his chest, and making a pained face.

"Holy shit, Dr. Meadows." Phil gulped in air. "You really shouldn't sneak up on a guy in a morgue."

Danica had a slightly concerned look on her face but couldn't help laughing a little. "Oh, Phil, I'm so sorry. I didn't mean to scare you." She reached out a hand and put it on his shoulder in a move to comfort him. "Are you okay?"

Finn smiled at Mila, who was chuckling behind a hand.

Phil smiled, then laughed. "I almost shit my pants, but I'll be okay." He took a breath and quickly closed out the first-person shooter game he had been playing, then held out a hand to Finn and Mila. "Hey, I'm Phil. You must be Dr. Meadows' friends, Finn and Mila, right?"

Finn shook hands with the gangly man. "That's right. It's nice to meet you, Phil. Care for a chew?" He pulled the box of Charleston Chew Minis from his pocket and shook the box.

"Um, yeah. Sure." Phil seemed a little confused by the offer but took the small handful that Finn dumped out for him. He tossed one in his mouth and chewed it for a second before his face lit up and he smiled, revealing chocolate on one of his teeth. "Hey, these things are great."

"They're his favorite, he says they taste even better melted into his coffee," Mila said, reaching out to shake hands as well.

Phil had the chews in his right hand, so he offered his left, making Mila switch. They shook awkwardly.

"Nice to meet you. Dr. Meadows talks about you all the time." He then dropped a couple of the chews into a steaming styrofoam cup sitting on the desk.

Finn felt a sharp talon in the small of his back, and he slipped a few of the chews inside his coat and felt Penny grab them before she let out a small coo of appreciation.

Phil took a sip of his melted-chew-flavored coffee and smiled like he had found the answer to cold fusion. "Holy shit. You're on to something here."

Mila glanced at Danica. "How much time do you spend down here? I thought you worked in pediatrics."

Danica blushed ever so slightly. "I have lunch with him sometimes. It's nice and quiet down here, and Phil's got me hooked on Babylon 5, so we'll watch an episode together during lunch."

Finn watched Mila glance from Danica to the awkward guy, who was trying to drink the hot coffee/chew concoction a little too fast. When she glanced back at Danica, Mila's face was filled with mischief.

He wasn't entirely sure what she was thinking, but he had a pretty good idea.

"Really?" Mila drew the word out, the corner of her lip going up in a bit of a smirk, and her eyes sparkling.

Danica glanced at Phil, who had just spilled some of the coffee on his lab coat and was trying to wipe it off with a piece of paper from his desk, completely unaware of the conversation.

She gave a sigh of defeat and turned back to Mila.

"Really," was all she said, but for some reason that Finn couldn't understand, that seemed to make Mila giddy.

Phil tossed the paper into the overflowing trash can beside the desk and turned back to the group, a cheery smile on his face. "You guys want to see the body?"

For some reason, that made Finn laugh. "I would love to, Phil. Thanks. I don't suppose you have his belongings here as well, do you?"

"Yeah."

He crossed the office to a metal cupboard and opened it with a small key that he fished from his pocket. On the shelves were about half a dozen plastic bags containing folded clothes and other belongings. Each space in the cupboard had a number that corresponded to one of the body lockers on the wall in the main room.

Phil pulled out a bag from the number 6 space. "Here you go."

He handed it to Mila, who inspected the contents through the clear plastic. There wasn't much, just a phone with dried blood on its screen, three rings, two of which had a gold chain through them, a cheap digital watch, and a wallet. The contents of the wallet had been removed and placed in a smaller Ziploc bag inside the larger one: about four dollars in cash, two rewards cards for grocery stores, and an ID from Wisconsin identifying the man as Peter Diver.

Finn immediately leaned in to inspect the rings but couldn't feel any magic whatsoever from them. They were just simple, gold rings, though one had a diamond set into it. The rings on the chain looked like a woman's engagement ring and wedding ring, and the other was a gold ring, sized for a man.

"Come on, he's in here." Phil led the way out into the main room and walked to the locker numbered 6.

"I have a feeling this is going to be way creepier than I thought," Mila said to Danica.

"It won't be so bad," her friend said, putting an arm around Mila's shoulder as they walked. "Most of the blood has been drained, so the body will be pretty clean-looking at this point."

Mila's face went a little white. "I don't know if that's better or worse."

Finn smiled and patted her shoulder reassuringly.

Phil, not noticing any of Mila's discomfort, pulled the door open and slid out the tray holding the dead man in one quick motion.

Mila gulped and turned a little green. Finn had to agree with her reaction. The man was naked and covered in bite marks that were nearly four inches across. Some were only perforated holes where the teeth had punctured the skin, but there was also quite a bit of flesh missing where the hounds had taken bigger bites from him, leaving huge holes in his body.

Finn shuddered when he remembered that Danica had told him the victim was still alive when he had arrived at the hospital, only to die a little while later. The pain must have been unbearable.

"Say hello to Peter Diver, everyone." Phil waved a hand over the mutilated body, his demeanor completely unaffected by the dead man in front of him.

There wasn't much they could get from the body, but Finn did feel the residual magic from the wounds Danica had mentioned, and it matched what he had felt coming from the hellhounds at the menagerie. This was not some random wolf attack or a cover-up; it was exactly what it looked like—a hellhound attack. And from the variation of the wound sizes, it looked like there had been multiple hounds.

Finn made eye contact with Danica, and ever so slightly nodded toward the door.

"Hey, Phil," Danica said, switching to the sweet voice she used when trying to get someone to do something for her. "I was going to get a cup of coffee. You want to come with me?"

He held up his styrofoam cup, which was still half-full. "I'm good. Just got one a little bit ago."

Finn rolled his eyes. This guy was denser than a neutron star.

"Well, I was going to get one for Finn and Mila too, and I was hoping you could help me carry them." She walked over and took him by the arm, gently guiding him toward the doors while she spoke.

"Oh, okay." He turned to Finn and Mila. "Will you two be okay for a few minutes?"

"They'll be fine," Danica answered before looking over her shoulder and telling them, "We'll be back in ten minutes." Then she pushed the swinging door open and led Phil out into the hall.

Finn waited a few seconds to be sure they were gone.

"She's a sharp one."

"Well, she is a doctor," Mila said matter-of-factly. "She just plays at being the pretty girl who doesn't know which way is up. I keep telling her she doesn't need to put on an act just to get a guy's attention. Though, I have noticed her doing it less and less. Maybe she and Phil are hitting it off...somehow." She laughed. "He is an odd dude."

Finn turned to see that she had gotten over her initial bout of queasiness, though she still wasn't looking directly at the body.

"Well, I don't see anything of use on the body." He held his jacket open. "Penny, you want to take a look and see if you can find any trace of the stone skin ring on him?"

A muffled chirp sounded from his jacket, and Penny scurried out onto his chest, then up onto his shoulder. She shook herself out, flapping her wings a few times, seeming to enjoy the feeling after riding in her hammock. She hopped down onto the tray holding the body and began sniffing. She closed her eyes, glowing with faint blue magic, weaving some unseen spell.

"Let's see what we have in the bag," Finn suggested to Mila, leading her to a small, stainless steel tray on a stand beside one of the dissection tables.

Mila emptied the bag onto the tray but stopped him from touching anything.

"Let me grab us some gloves, just in case."

She found boxes of latex gloves on a counter and grabbed a small pair for herself and a large set for Finn. They took a second to get the gloves on, Finn nearly ripping his open because his hands were so big. Once their hands were protected, they went about seeing what they could find on Peter Diver.

"I don't think this is his current address." Finn held up the Wisconsin ID before tossing it on the tray.

Mila picked up the cell phone and hit the power button. To their surprise, it still had a charge but went into a booting sequence, so she put it to the side and picked up the rings on the chain.

"Must be an ex or something," Finn suggested.

She shook her head. "She probably died. You don't wear your ex's rings, but you do wear your deceased spouse's rings. Poor guy probably lost her recently if he was still wearing them."

The phone let off a chime, and they both glanced over to see the home screen through the rust-brown of dried blood. There was a distinct ear print in the blood from where he must have called 911 after the attack.

"It's locked, and I don't want to try to guess the passcode. Most phones have a lockout if you put it in wrong too many times." Mila said, frowning at their bad luck.

"Chi! Sqee shi chree," Penny said with a shrug.

"You think that would work?" Finn asked, taking the phone and walking over to the body.

Penny lifted the dead man's finger, and Finn pressed the button at the bottom of the phone with it. There was a click, and the phone opened.

"That's why I keep you around." Finn smiled at Penny, who gave him a good eye-roll.

"I can't really see anything through the blood. We'll need to wipe it off, but I don't want to disturb any evidence." Mila frowned.

"Well, the cops aren't going to need this to find out what happened since they think it was a wolf attack. Case closed. But *we* need it to find the hounds, so more people don't get hurt." Finn gave her a shrug. "I would rather be right than lawful. Besides," he pulled his phone out of his pocket, "we can replace it with mine. I still haven't used it once since we got it."

Mila gave him the face she used when she knew he was right but still didn't like it.

He smiled and went to the counter, finding some alcohol swabs, and began cleaning the blood from the phone. When he was done, they had to use Peter's finger to open the phone again.

"That's going to be a problem." Finn went through the menus till he found the password settings, but he quickly ran into an issue. "Shit, I can't change it without entering the original."

Mila took the phone from him. "Hang on. I think I have an idea."

He watched her fiddle with the settings for a few minutes, then take a glove off and press her finger to the home button a few times, rolling it back and forth. She smiled and hit the power button, shutting off the screen. She hit it again, and the phone lit up but was locked. When she pressed her finger to the button, the phone unlocked.

"I updated the finger scanner. Don't have the code, but the phone now recognizes my print." She beamed, obviously proud of herself.

Finn looked across the room at Penny. "Check out the brains on this one."

Penny just closed her eyes and shook her head, folding her arms and placing a hand over her face.

"Well, I am a doctor," Mila argued haughtily.

"And a clever one at that." He smiled, leaning in to get a look at the phone.

They scrolled through his contacts, finding only a few numbers. Each was saved under a single letter as the name; O, D, J, and K.

"Well, that isn't very helpful. We need to know where he lived, or at least where he went all the time," Finn said.

Mila went back to the home screen and opened the map app. She pulled down the menu and smiled.

"I noticed on my phone that after I'd used my GPS for a while, it automatically understood where I lived, and labeled my house without me telling it to. Looks like the same thing happened to mister Diver."

Finn leaned back, looking her over with a raised eyebrow. "Damn. You really are smart."

She rolled her eyes and slipped the phone into her pocket, then started putting things back into the plastic bag. When she was done, she took Finn's unused phone and dropped it in as well.

"Shiriir!" Penny tooted, a flame shooting from a nostril in excitement.

Finn nodded. "Good. We have an address too, so it looks like this case is in the bag."

"What did she find?" Mila asked.

"She smells the stone ring all over him, though it's faint since he wasn't wearing it. This is definitely our guy."

Mila stepped over and held out a fist to Penny. "Good work, Penn. Looks like Finn is the only one who hasn't got them doctor brains."

Penny fist-bumped her and hooted a laugh at Finn's frown.

CHAPTER ELEVEN

After Phil and Danica returned, Finn and Mila said they were done with the examination, and thanked Phil for his time. As they were leaving the funeral home, attendants showed up to take the body and its belongings. Danica told Phil that she would see him on her next shift and gave him a friendly wave. Finn swore he saw her give him a wink.

Feeling confident that they had the case well in hand, Finn suggested they go have a drink, and leave the visit to Peter Diver's house for the morning. He had a delivery coming to the bar that night, and he didn't want to miss it.

They stopped at the condo and saw a moving truck parked out front, although from the late hour, Finn figured Simon and Becky had had the movers park it there so they wouldn't have to find a space in the morning rush. The girls went to their respective rooms and changed into something more appropriate for a night out, while Finn and Penny watched the beginning of *McLintock!* for the third time that week.

Penny was pretty much over John Wayne, but she didn't have anything better to do, so she spread out on the couch beside Finn. The girls were ready just about the time that Louise and Dev move into McLintock's house.

Finn grabbed a small red vest that said Service Animal in white embroidery and handed it to Penny. She slipped it on as Mila and Danica laughed.

"I can't believe Danny lets you get away with that." Mila shook her head with a big smile on her face. "Penny is obviously not a service animal."

"He said it was fine as long as no one complained, and this lets her hang out at the table with us. Sometimes you have to just take the small victories." He stood, and Penny hopped onto his shoulder, adjusting the vest.

"Chi shiri," she said happily.

Finn barked a laugh. "She says you two got dressed up, why not her?"

Mila laughed. "I guess you have me there, Penny. You do look pretty cute."

Penny smiled, her head shrinking into her shoulders as she waved the compliment away in embarrassment.

The girls had chosen to wear their magic boots, as Finn liked to think of them. Four-inch heels did amazing things to Mila's normally four-ten frame, and Danica, having longer feet, went with five-inch heels, putting her only a couple of inches below Finn's height.

They walked the three blocks to the Refinery. It was a nice place, but not so upscale they had to dress up, but the girls made the effort anyway.

Mila wore dark, fitted jeans and a flowing red top that hung off one shoulder, which contrasted her black hair and tanned skin perfectly. The addition of the knee-high boots put her over the edge of stylish without much effort.

Danica was similarly dressed in light blue skinny jeans and a white flowing top with both shoulders cut out, showing off her flawless, pale skin. Her boots were really just tall heels that came up to her ankle, but she insisted that they were called ankle boots. When pressed, she couldn't explain the difference except that they "look like boots...sort of".

Finn decided it wasn't worth the argument.

He, of course, just wore blue jeans and his customary black t-shirt beneath his brown leather bomber jacket, like always.

He held the door for the women as they entered the bar, and Penny adjusted her vest one more time before she and Finn followed. The bar was not all that busy, but it usually wasn't on weekdays; however, there was a small group of people there for Karaoke. Danica went to claim them a table up near the front of the little stage, while Mila and Finn went for drinks.

"Ho there, Finn," Danny the bartender greeted, his heavy Scottish accent cutting through the warbling voices of the duet on stage. "Mila, always a pleasure, darlin'. What can I be gettin' far ye?"

"Hello, Danny. We'll have the usual. Danica too." She leaned on the bar, able to get her elbows up on the top with the extra four inches from her boots.

"I'll take a beer as well tonight," Finn added, leaning on the bar next to Mila.

Penny, riding Finn's shoulder, was eyeing the bowl of

peanuts a few feet away on the bar, but knew better than to go after them.

Danny had made it quite clear that she was not allowed on the bar top when he had scooped her up and handed her back to Finn on one of their visits. The brazen action had almost led to a burnt and bitten hand. Luckily, Penny was sharp enough not to bite the man that could kick them out forever, but she still wanted the peanuts.

Danny quickly made gin and tonics for Mila and Danica and poured a double shot of rye whiskey and a pint for Finn. When he placed the drinks in front of them, he also scooped out a fresh bowl of peanuts from the large plastic container behind the bar and served them up with a wink at Penny.

"Ere ya go. You'll be wantin' ta start a tab, I'm assumin'?" he asked, rolling his head and cracking his neck.

"That would be great, Danny. Thanks." Mila gave him a big smile and picked up the two G&Ts and headed for the table where Danica was waving to them.

Finn picked up the whiskey and beer in one hand and the bowl of peanuts in the other and gave Danny a half-salute with the bowl before following Mila.

The couple on the stage finished up their song to applause, though it was definitely not a reflection of their talent, more of their willingness to get up there in the first place.

When they reached the table, Danica had the songbook open, and several small slips of paper in front of her to write down her selections.

"How about *'We Will Rock You'*?" she suggested, then her eyes lit up. "No, wait."

She quickly wrote down the song code and flipped the page so Mila couldn't see what she had selected.

"You're going to love this one."

Mila took a long sip of her drink while giving Danica the eye. "Somehow, I doubt that."

Penny chuckled and slipped off Finn's shoulder to dive into the bowl of peanuts. She slithered in head-first, displacing several nuts until her head came up and out of the bowl on the opposite side, her cheeks full as she crunched away. Peanut skins and dust clung to her face, but she didn't care. She stretched out her arms and rested them on the rim of the bowl like it was a bathtub.

Finn and the girls watched her defile the bowl of nuts. She did the same thing every time, but it never got less weird to watch.

"I don't know how she stays so skinny. If I ate that entire bowl of peanuts, I would have to unbutton my pants just from the sheer volume of nuts in my belly." Mila shook her head in disbelief as Penny shoved another handful of nuts in her mouth and chewed them loudly.

"She burns a lot of calories using her magic," Finn said, taking a sip of whiskey as Danica went up to give the DJ the slip of paper with her song selection on it. "Imagine if she were bigger. She would eat us out of house and home! Hell, she might even eat the house and home."

Penny shot him a dark look but didn't stop eating.

"Mila!" Danica shouted over the noise of the small crowd, waving for her to come up on stage. "We're on."

Mila sighed. "I hate it when she picks the song without telling me what it is beforehand."

Finn laughed. "No, you don't. You just like to complain about it."

She lightly smacked his arm but smiled as she slid off her stool and nearly skipped to the stage. She took one of the microphones and gave Danica a fake glare.

Danica gave a laugh in return and, right on cue, started *Don't Stop Me Now*.

"Toooonight, I'm gonna have myself a real good time."

Mila burst out laughing at her song choice, but Danica continued. Mila recovered just in time to sing the chorus with her.

"Don't. Stop. Me. Now." The tempo doubled, and they sang the lead together. *"Cause I'm having a good time, I'm having a good time!"*

Finn smiled, and Penny repositioned herself to see the stage better from her peanut bath. Both women had pretty good singing voices, even if they tended to choose songs that didn't exactly fit their range, but their enthusiasm made up for any mistakes, and the crowd loved them.

Right around the first musical interlude, Finn felt a small hand pulling on his jacket sleeve, and he looked down to see a small, muscular girl in a green hoodie looking up at him with a smile.

Her features were a little sharp and mature for as small as she was, and it took Finn a second to recognize her.

"Remmy?" he asked. Not having seen the little goblin with a concealment spell before, he wasn't entirely sure it was her.

She smiled even bigger, her sharp nose wrinkling at the bridge. "Yep. Good to see you again, My Lord."

Finn had saved the goblin's life a few weeks before

while going to meet with a Naga to gather components for the favor he'd subsequently given to Mila. The little goblin and her tribe had then made a deal with the Naga for mutual protection in the dangerous underworld below Denver's streets.

"What did I say about that 'My Lord' shit?" Finn frowned down at her.

She blushed slightly. "Sorry, Finn," she grumbled, climbing up onto the stool next to his.

She slid a brown paper wrapped package onto the table and snatched a small handful of peanuts from the bowl with Penny in it, stuffing them into her mouth before Penny could stop her. She then giggled at the face Penny made, her mischievous goblin nature coming out in full.

"I didn't realize you came up top," Finn said, getting Remmy back on track. "Not that it isn't nice to see you."

"I come up when the pay is good." She smirked. "Deliveries pay pretty well, especially when I get tipped." She raised an eyebrow at him.

He chuckled and pulled a small wad of cash from his back pocket. "I take it this is my order from the leathersmith?"

Remmy's eyes were locked on the wad of bills, but she nodded. "He said you would be here, so I waited outside till I saw you come in." She slid the box closer to him.

Finn slipped a couple of twenties from the wad. "What do you use money for, out of curiosity? Don't you spend most of your time hunting in the caverns?"

"Yeah, but my tribe likes to have some luxuries from up top." She gave a shrug. "It's not like we're sized properly to form a permanent community up here."

Finn cocked his head in thought. All the goblins he had ever met preferred to live underground like their ancestors. Or so he'd thought. "Are you saying that you and your people don't want to be underground anymore?"

Remmy bobbed her shoulders up and down a few times as she thought about it. "I mean, it would just be nice to be able to come out sometimes. Maybe have a nice farm or something. Plus, some reliable internet would be awesome."

Finn frowned and handed Remmy the whole stack of bills. "Here, take it and get you and your people something nice."

Her already large eyes went wide. "Really? Thank you, sir!"

Finn gave her a hard look and slowly reached for the stack of bills.

Remmy jerked the bills out of his reach. "I mean, thank you, *Finn.*"

He smiled. "That's better."

She slid off the stool and waved. "Thanks. I'll talk to you later, Finn. I hope she likes it." She slipped between two patrons and was out the front door in a few seconds.

Danica and Mila were finishing up the song, holding their mics and singing into one another's faces, smiles so big they could hardly get the words out.

Penny eyed the package as Finn slid it to the space in front of Mila's stool. "Chi shi?"

He smiled. "You'll have to wait for her to open it."

She huffed but didn't argue. Instead, she slid deeper into the peanuts and shoved a handful in her mouth.

The girls finished up, and Finn joined the rest of the bar in applause as they made their way back to the table.

"Well done." He was all smiles as they took their seats. "Whoever wrote that song must have had you two in mind."

Danica laughed. "It was Queen. And I'm pretty sure they had something else in mind at the time."

"Queen who?" Finn knit his brows. He didn't think there were so many monarchs on *Earth* that one of them would also be a singer.

"Just Queen. What's in the box?" Mila asked, lifting the brown paper package and looking for a label of some kind.

Finn was still not sure what land this queen ruled, but he let it go, his excitement over the gift winning out.

"It's a present for you. A thank-you if you will, but also something I think you'll need if you're going to continue working with Penny and me."

Mila smiled and tore into the paper like it was Christmas morning. Danica nearly bounced with excitement, waiting to see what it was. Mila got the paper off and opened the box. Her face froze in a half-smile as she stared inside.

Danica noticed the change immediately and became concerned. "Are you okay? What is it?"

Mila slowly looked up and met Finn's eyes, her cheeks nearly glowing red with embarrassment. "I didn't think you would be so forward, but if this is the kind of stuff you're into, I guess I can go with it. I mean, it's really nice quality, but I just never thought…" She trailed off, unable to find the words.

Finn was completely baffled by her response. He

wondered if the leathersmith had messed up the order, but before he could inspect it, Danica lost her patience and slid the box over to take a look for herself.

"Holy shit, Finn." Danica slid a finger over the tight stitching. "You are not messing around. This is top-quality workmanship."

She reached into the package and lifted out a black leather corset. It wasn't a traditional corset with boning, but it was shaped like one and had a zipper running up the front, hidden by a flap. The detail work was intricate on the edges, but the main panels were smooth and shone slightly in the bar lights.

Mila went an even deeper shade of red and peered around to see if anyone was looking. "Why would you get me lingerie?"

Danica and Finn both looked at her like she was insane, and Penny rolled from side to side in her bowl, holding her stomach and laughing.

"It's not lingerie, dummy." Danica shook her head. "It's a battle harness. Like what Finn wears. See, look here on the back."

She laid the corset down and began to point out the incorporated pockets with flaps that snapped shut with magnets sewn into the supple leather.

"There are slots for healing potions, and this looks like a holster for Gram." She pointed out a hard leather band that would sit at the small of her back where the golden sword would fit. "This is a masterpiece. I'm not going to lie; I'm super jealous."

The red had started to fade from Mila's cheeks as she

realized what she was looking at. She picked it up and examined it more closely.

"Okay, now that I know what it is, it's pretty badass. But why does it have to be leather? I'll look like a dominatrix." She blushed again.

"Well, you already have the Mithril armor, so I didn't need to get you a material that would protect you," Finn explained, trying to guess what a dominatrix was. "But I also knew that it would probably take quite a bit of damage. If you look along the edges, that scrollwork is not just for decoration; it's a runic spell script that will allow the leather to grow back if it gets damaged. That kind of spell works best on organic material, so I went with leather."

"Plus, it's super sexy," Danica said with a sly smile.

That made Mila flush once again.

CHAPTER TWELVE

They spent the rest of the night singing Karaoke, drinking, and having a good time. Finn was starting to realize just how important spending time with friends was. In his previous life, before crash-landing on this strange and wondrous world, he had spent all his time with Penny, as they wound up in a different place every few days. They never put down any roots or made friends that were more than just a means to an end for their current hunt.

A part of himself had longed for companionship, and Penny filled a lot of that need, which allowed him to lie to himself and say everything was all right. Now that he had Mila and Danica in his life, he was beginning to realize what a sour old jackass he used to be. Even Penny was doing better now that she had a shoulder to sit on that wasn't always his.

She was bonding with Mila in a way Finn had never seen from the faerie dragon in all the years they had been together. Sometimes he would come out into the living room to see the two of them napping together on the couch, and it would always make him smile.

They headed home late that night, the girls each hanging onto one of his arms to keep their balance as their heads swam in a warm, drunken haze. They sang Queen songs the entire three-block walk that took a little longer than usual, as they took a few minutes to dance under the streetlights and belt out power ballads. Finn smiled and let them sing, and he and Penny would laugh when one or the other messed up the lyrics and had to start over.

By three in the morning, he had put the two women to bed, not arguing when they both insisted on sleeping in Mila's room. He gave each of them some ibuprofen and a big glass of water, which he made them drink before letting them fall into bed fully clothed. He took a few minutes to remove their boots and cover them up with a spare blanket from the cedar chest at the foot of Mila's bed. Then he watched the two of them cuddle up and begin snoring immediately before he went out into the living room and cracked open another beer from the fridge.

He flipped the TV on to finish watching *McLintock!*, to Penny's annoyance. She would much rather watch the finale to *Survivor*, but Finn just couldn't make himself watch it; there was no story there. She resigned herself to more of the Duke and curled up beside him.

"I like it here, Penny," he mused as he watched the Duke brawl at the mine. "I feel like we finally made it home, you know?"

Penny looked up at him, her face serious as she thought about that. Finally, she gave a single nod. "Squee shir." A single ring of smoke puffed from her nostril, and she laid her head back down to watch the movie.

Finn nodded. "Yeah, Mila is the main reason, but we have a purpose here. Out there, when we were finding treasures, it was fun, but that was it. There was no real goal for me. Here, we have a goal, a job to protect this great ship from the ravages of powerful dwarven artifacts. It's a good feeling knowing that what we do here makes a difference."

"Shiri cheesh. Sqeuee chi rich." She shrugged.

Finn thought about that. "Well, I guess protecting *Earth* isn't the only goal. We do still have to find you a hoard so you can finally lay your eggs."

A smile crossed her lips, but she didn't say anything else.

Finn sighed in frustration. "Look, the deal between us was that I would help you find a hoard, and I understand that your kind are very secretive, but I need a hint here. I'm pretty dense, but not so dense that I haven't figured out that you're not looking for precious metals and jewels. We've had plenty of those over the years. So, what is it that you need to gather? Just a hint."

She lifted her head and gave him a narrow gaze as if trying to decide something. "Shnick," she said finally, shaking her head before turning back to the movie.

"Fine. Keep your secrets." He took another sip of beer. "But at least let me know if we're getting close."

She reached out and patted his leg. "Chi chi."

They fell asleep on the couch. The movie ended, and the streaming service logo bounced around on the screen.

Finn came awake suddenly as if no time had passed at all, but the room was now full of early morning light. The banging sound of furniture being moved came through the wall, and Becky's voice shouted for someone to be careful.

Finn got up, stretching after sleeping in a sitting position all night, and began making breakfast. By the time the coffee was done and the bacon was frying, Mila and Danica came stumbling out of Mila's room.

"Good morning," Finn said, flipping the frying meat, and dropping a dollop of pancake batter into another skillet. "How do you two feel?"

"Like I was hit by a truck," Mila said, and Danica groaned in agreement, pulling two mugs from the cupboard and pouring herself and Mila some coffee.

"I think we should get over to Peter's house this morning and wrap this whole thing up. How long do you think you'll need to get ready?"

Mila slumped onto a stool at the kitchen island and sipped on her coffee. "Not until I've had at least three of these. And a shower. And some pancakes."

Over the course of the morning, Danica recovered faster than Mila, partly because she was an elf, but mostly because she was a lot taller and bigger. After breakfast, Danica went and changed into her work clothes and waved goodbye to everyone as she slipped out the door, back to her normal, chipper self.

"I hate how she can do that," Mila complained, still looking like death warmed over.

"You could just take a healing potion," Finn suggested.

Mila blinked a few times, letting that sink in. "Why didn't I think of that?"

She got up and went to the safe where they kept their valuables and punched in the code. A second later, she was holding a red vial, working the stopper. She downed the contents in one long gulp, tilting her head back to be sure she got it all, then smacked her lips a few times.

She walked back to the island, a look of euphoria on her face, and plopped back down on the stool.

The healing potions took a few minutes to work fully, making them nearly useless in combat, but the effects when a little time could be afforded were extraordinary. Within two minutes, she looked like she'd had a full night's sleep, the bags gone from under her eyes, and she sat up straighter.

She sucked in a refreshing breath. "Holy shit, that's some good stuff."

Finn chuckled. "Yeah, they work like a charm, but they're a little expensive for an everyday hangover cure."

"Oh god, I didn't even think about that! Well, that's one way to spend a grand or so. Good thing we're operating a gold mine." She laughed and winked. "I'm going to get ready."

Finn decided he needed a shower as well and used Danica's while Mila got ready in her room. When Mila emerged, Finn was happy to see that she had worn the corset and that it fit her like a glove. She didn't comment, but he could see that she had stored Gram and a few potions in the leather pockets designed for the slim, test tube-style bottles. She had thrown her short black jacket on over the corset, and the leather matched perfectly. Finn had to admit she looked like a proper badass.

Thirty minutes after breakfast, they were in the Hellcat and pulling onto the freeway. Mila pulled up the address on Peter's phone and put it into the navigation system on her own phone, then punched the gas and rocketed into the fast lane with a guttural growl from all eight cylinders.

Finn took the time on the short drive to scroll through the messages on Peter's phone, seeing if there was anything of importance. There were text threads with each of the four saved contacts, but it seemed like they were talking in code. He couldn't make heads or tails of most of it. But when he got to the texts from J, he started to understand a little better.

It looked like this J was his main contact about the hounds. There was talk of money changing hands for the pups, and timeframes that could have been in months or days but were only mentioned in numbers.

"Interesting," Finn commented, scrolling through the texts. Penny sat on his shoulder, reading along with him.

"What's interesting?" Mila changed lanes and passed a box truck that was hogging the left lane.

"It looks like this J person was paying Peter a hundred grand to deliver the hound, but Peter wanted more." He scrolled down and kept going, his eyes getting wide. "Holy shit, they had a falling out, and J called it off, then about two weeks ago, Peter contacted J again and said that he would take the original offer, but J would have to take the hound pups as well. The last text was received two days ago. J told Peter they would come pick up the hounds, but that he had better not try anything."

"Sounds like they had a strained relationship at best." Mila took the next exit, slowing down for the backed-up traffic. "Does that mean the hounds will be gone?"

Finn shrugged. "If they are, then they were gone last

night too. Not much we can do about it until we get there and check."

They pulled onto the main drag and went about a mile until the navigation had them turn into a residential area. It was one of those cookie-cutter neighborhoods that had sprung up during the fifties; small houses packed in tight, but with backyards and little driveways.

Mila wove her way through the old streets, turning down a dead-end street that ran straight into a set of train tracks that cut through the neighborhood. She pulled into the drive of the last house on the left and turned the car off.

The house was a faded pastel blue, with metal awnings over the windows that looked about thirty years out of date. The house was a small one-story thing that couldn't have been much more than a thousand square feet and was in dire need of some updates. A one-car garage was attached, with a chain-link fence around the backyard, which was backed up against some dead-looking trees.

"Doesn't really scream 'master thief,' does it?" She raised an eyebrow at the police tape crossing the front door. One of the yellow ribbons had come loose and was waving in the wind. "I didn't think about the police being here. What if they already found the hound?"

Finn shook his head. "Not a chance. Those things are magically shielded, or Preston would have found them right away. I'm betting there's some kind of concealment spell on them. But there's only one way to find out."

He climbed out of the car, Mila following him. As soon as he was outside, he could smell a strong odor of lilacs and something a little more earthy, like a mushroom or root vegetable of some kind, a sure sign that some sort of magic was in play.

"Can you smell anything?" he asked Penny, who closed her eyes and took in a deep breath.

After a second, she nodded and pointed. "Shirir chi chi."

"She says she can smell the ring coming from around back." Finn led the way around the garage and through the gate in the chain-link fence. "That's a good sign that the hound is still here."

"You guys can just smell magic?" Mila asked, closing the gate behind herself.

"Not exactly, but sort of." Finn smiled over his shoulder at her as they walked the length of the small, one-car garage. "You can smell the lilacs, right?"

She stopped and took a sniff. Then a deeper inhalation, closing her eyes to enhance her sense of smell. She nodded. "Faintly. Is that what magic smells like?"

"Some of it. It changes depending on who is using it; we all have our own scent when we perform a spell. Mine smells mostly like pine trees, and Penny's...well, Penny's changes depending on the spell, but she's unique."

They rounded the garage, and Finn saw a backyard that looked like it hadn't been mowed in about a year. There was a path beaten down from the back door to a small shed at the back of the property, but everywhere else looked like an untamed jungle.

"I'm going to check out the shed. See if you can see anything through the house's windows," he suggested, then started to tromp through the foot-and-a-half-tall grass.

"Why would you ask the short one to look into

windows?" Mila complained, but she was smiling when he looked back.

He gave a chuckle. "You could try jumping."

She gave him the finger, which made him laugh harder.

With a roll of her eyes, she turned and started making her way to the back of the house.

Finn flattened a path to the shed as he cut across the yard. It was newer than the house by many years, but it was still in pretty bad shape. Some of the wood around the bottom was rotting out, and the door didn't exactly hang straight. There was a small padlock on it, but that seemed like all the security. He took a second to see if he could detect any wards on the door but felt nothing, so he reached out for the lock.

He gripped the metal in his fist, feeling for its composition with a small shot of dwarven magic. His eyes turned light gray as the magic flowed, and the smell of pine filled the backyard. Once he knew what the lock was made of, it was a simple matter of using his power to change its composition ever so slightly.

His hand glowed purple for a few heartbeats, then he withdrew the power and checked the lock. It had lost its metallic shine and was flaking at the edges.

Finn smiled up at Penny. "Nothing like a few hundred years of oxidation in a few seconds to compromise the thing's integrity."

He had used a considerable amount of power to achieve the feat, but he wasn't worried about needing much of his magic here and deemed it an acceptable risk.

He squeezed the lock, and it crumbled in his hand, turning to powder at the slight pressure. He wiped his palm on his jeans and undid the latch, swinging the door open on squeaky hinges.

The interior of the shed was in the same shape as the outside, and aside from a rusted-out lawnmower and a barrel full of yard tools, the place was empty. He stepped inside to see if there was maybe a trapdoor or something in the floor.

As he was moving the old lawnmower, Mila let out a scream of pain and surprise.

CHAPTER THIRTEEN

Mila watched Finn slog through the dense grass and turned to the house. The back of the house was in far worse shape than the front. Paint was peeling off in sheets, and rot had taken large sections of the siding, leaving dark brown holes that smelled strongly of earth. The concrete steps up to the back door were crumbling on the edges to the point that the iron railing had fallen out and was tangled in overgrown grass. The steps themselves seemed solid enough, though.

She had to high-step through the grass, unable to force her way through like Finn had, and made her way to the back door. Climbing the steps, she cupped her hands around her face and pressed them to the glass window of the door. The dim interior took her eyes a few seconds to adapt to, and when she could finally make out more than a few random shapes, she saw a kitchen that hadn't been updated since the seventies. The room was fairly clean and seemed to be in order. There was an arched doorway that led to a small living room, where she could see an old, yellow couch and a stained La-Z-Boy© with a small table and lamp beside it.

She tried the door but found it locked. Blowing a loose strand of black hair from her face, she looked around the backyard one more time. She saw Finn standing at the shed, holding the padlock in his hand. The smell of pine filled the yard, and she saw his hand glowing purple even in the daylight.

"I wish I could do that," she grumbled, looking over her shoulder at the locked back door.

Out of the corner of her eye, she saw a cellar door that she hadn't noticed before jutting out of the back of the house, but when she looked directly at it, it sort of slipped out of view, leaving the sight of more overgrown grass.

A tingle went down her spine. She realized immediately what was happening.

This was magic, and she was able to see it.

Granted, only from a side angle, but still.

When she tried looking from the corner of her eye again, she could still see it, unlike when she had tried a second time in the past and it hadn't worked. Finn had told her that now that she knew about magic, her peabrain would start to wake up. He'd warned her that it might take years, but here she was showing signs of awakening after only a few weeks. She had always been a bit of an over-achiever.

A huge smile crossed her face, and she slowly made her way down the porch steps, feeling out each one as she focused on the cellar door in the corner of her eye. She nearly fell over, tripping on the tall grass, but eventually, she got there. Standing right in front of the cellar's double steel doors on a steep incline, she felt disoriented when she looked directly at it and it vanished.

A fly began buzzing around her, but she was so focused on the fact that she was able to see the door when she turned her head that she didn't notice it.

Keeping her head turned nearly ninety degrees to the right and focusing on the blurry image of the doors, she knelt down and reached out a hand, searching for a handle.

The buzzing of the fly grew in volume as the insect flew next to her ear. She waved a hand at it, but it persisted.

She bit her lip in concentration. She never realized how hard it was to judge distance from your periphery. She had a few false starts, but she scooted forward and reached out one last time.

Her hand was almost to the handle when the fly bit her on the ear.

She let out a scream and stumbled backward, her hand flying up to her throbbing ear. She had never been bitten by an insect in her entire life, and the sensation was far more intense than she could have imagined. She blinked back tears as she felt the lobe of her ear. It was swelling and throbbing with heat.

The fly buzzed right in her face, somehow seeming sorry, but still insistent on getting her attention.

"What the fuck, man? Why did you bite me?" she pleaded with what she could now see was a horsefly about the size of her pinkie's first two knuckles put together.

Its thick black and gray body bounced up and down, trying to communicate something to her.

A crashing sound made her jump, and she spun to see Finn barreling out of the shed with so much force that he half ripped the door off its hinges when he hit it with his shoulder. Fragar was out and unfolded. The dwarf's eyes were wide as he scanned his surroundings, tearing through the yard with such force that clumps of grass went flying, with dirt still attached to the roots.

Penny had taken wing, circling the yard, looking for the enemy she assumed had to be there.

"What was it? The hound? Kashgar?" Finn was wild with the need to protect her.

"It was a fly," she said lamely, pointing to the large horsefly hovering in front of her.

Finn slowed to a stop like a train running out of steam. He blinked and raised an eyebrow at the insect. "A fly? Why did you scream?"

"It bit me!" She showed him her swollen lobe.

"Okay…" He leaned in to look at the small dribble of blood from the bite. "I mean, it looks pretty bad for a fly bite, but it's still just a fly."

Mila's lips tightened in a thin line as she frowned at his denseness. "You know how I get along with insects. That was the first time I've ever been bitten. It scared me." She rubbed her ear. "And it really, really hurt."

Penny swooped down and landed on Mila's shoulder. Reaching out a taloned hand, Penny gently touched the swollen earlobe. A cooling sensation flooded Mila, and she could smell berries. The pain faded away in seconds, replaced by a feeling of wholeness.

Penny removed her hand and patted Mila on the head. "Shir?" she asked in a gentle voice.

"She wants to know if that feels better," Finn translated.

Mila felt her ear again. It was swollen, and her fingertip

came away with a dab of blood on it, but the pain had vanished completely.

"Yeah, what did you do?"

Penny gave a series of chirp and clicks, her hands gesticulating as she got lost in the explanation.

Mila glanced at Finn when Penny finally quieted down.

He laughed. "She took the long way of saying that she can soothe emotions and pain with her magic. It's how she keeps me from going over the edge when my berserker rage kicks in."

"Oh," she held out a fist for Penny to bump. "Well, thanks, Penny."

Penny gave her a slight bow and bumped fists, then pointed at the fly. "Squee chir chi?"

Mila didn't know what she asked exactly, but she got the idea. "I don't know why it bit me. I was trying to open this cellar door, and it just freaked out."

"What cellar door?" Finn asked, looking around the backyard.

Penny focused on the ground and began to glow slightly blue as she tapped into her magic once again. Her eyes widened, and she glanced at Mila, giving her a thumbs-up before hopping off her shoulder and slowly approaching where Mila figured the edge of the doors was. Penny held her little hands up and began to glow brighter as she closed her eyes and focused.

Finn, still not seeing the concealed doors, squinted down at the area he knew they should be, and shook his head. "Damn, girl. How did you see that? I can't detect it at all."

Mila shrugged. "I don't know, I can just see it out of the corner of my eye, like when I first noticed your tattoos."

Her eyebrows rose with an idea, and she tried the trick on Finn. She turned her head so that he was in her peripheral vision and focused on the short hair on the side of his head. She smiled as she saw the deep blue runes that circled the back of his head like a wreath. It was the first time she'd seen them since they had first met, and they were as intricate as she remembered.

When she looked directly at him again, the runes vanished, and he looked the same as he had every day for the last few weeks.

She opened her mouth to say something when a loud popping sound made her jump back and instinctively reach for Gram.

Penny shook out her hand, kneeling in front of a set of steel doors that had not been there a moment before. "Chi chi." She frowned at her hand and shook it out again. "Shiri chi quee shee." A small jet of flame punctuated what Mila thought might have been a bunch of dragon f-bombs.

"Interesting," Finn mused, his eyebrow raised as he regarded the newly revealed doors. "She says the doors had a ward on them that would have hurt or more likely killed you if you touched them. Someone really didn't want this found. Looks like you owe your little fly buddy thanks."

Mila gulped, making a fist with the hand that she had almost touched the door with, and looked around for the fly, but it was gone. "That's frightening. What if I had tripped over it?"

"Not likely," Finn said, reaching down and grasping the now dispelled handle. "The spell would have kept you away subconsciously. I want to know how you made it over here in the first place. That ward should have made you forget what you were doing."

He pulled the door open before she could come up with a theory, and loud barking and howling turned her focus to the dark stairs leading down.

"Sounds like the hound is still here." She pulled Gram out but didn't activate the golden sword. "Maybe you should go first," she suggested.

Finn smiled and hefted Fragar before taking the steps one at a time in a crouched, ready position. He got to the bottom and fumbled around for a few seconds before flipping a switch. When golden light filled the darkness as the overhead lights came on, Finn's shoulders loosened, and he stood up.

"Come on down. She's still locked up."

Mila started down the stairs, and Penny hopped onto her shoulder for a ride.

The cellar was probably the nicest part of the house. The walls were white cinder block, and one corner of the room contained a cot, a small refrigerator, and a table with a TV and an ashtray with a couple of stubbed out butts in it. The rest of the large space was made up of chain-link kennels, about twenty in all. Aside from the blood that was dried all over the floor, it was pretty nice.

"What the fuck happened here?" Mila asked, noting that the smell of lilac had faded, now that they were out of the yard. She reasoned it was the spell on the cellar doors that had been causing the smell, but the pleasant aroma had been replaced with that of dog feces and stale cigarettes.

"This is where Peter was attacked," Finn said, stepping

up to the barking hound in the last cage. "You can see the trail where he pulled himself out into the yard and called the ambulance."

Mila glanced at the steps, and sure enough, there was dried blood all over the wooden risers. They had walked right through it and hadn't noticed because it was so dark. She noticed several bloody pawprints as well, indicating that a lot of large hounds had walked up the stairs after the attack.

She didn't know much about tracking, but the fact that all the prints were whole and not streaked made her think that they had calmly walked up the steps, as if they were following someone, and not fleeing.

The barking stopped, and Mila turned to see the hound for the first time in the flesh. After a second's consideration, she thought "flesh" might not be the right word.

She had seen the grainy video of the hound, but that was nothing compared to the specimen that stood before her in the cage. She was nearly as tall as Mila, and slim now that her pups had been born. Her eyes glowed red, but not with malice. Mila thought she detected a look of sadness in them.

But it was the hound's coat that really drew the eye.

Under the bare bulbs in the fixture on the ceiling, her fur had turned to white marble, thanks to the golden ring on her tail that glinted in the light. Mila could see veins of black and pink in her coat, and the effect made the animal look like a statue until she moved, and the illusion was broken. Then she would settle once again, and Mila would again question her authenticity.

"She's beautiful," Mila said, coming over to stand next

to Finn, who had squatted down to look the hound in the eyes.

"She is, but she's also quite upset, and if I had to guess, she could do with a little food. Hellhounds don't eat every day, but we don't know how long it's been since she was last fed. I have to say, the fact that she's so docile right now is surprising."

Finn reached out a hand to the hound sitting behind the fence, making gentle sounds. He almost had his fingers through the links when the hound bared her pointed teeth and lunged at him.

He jerked his hand back and barked a laugh. "Well, not all that docile, I guess. We need to distract her so I can get that ring off her tail. Hellhounds are tough, but not so tough I can't handle one if I have to. However, with her stone skin, I would probably lose a hand for my efforts."

Mila swept her eyes across the room and saw the small refrigerator near the cot and TV. She went over and opened it up, finding it stocked with raw cuts of beef still in the foam tray and plastic wrap of the local grocers.

Penny smiled and nodded, patting Mila on the head.

"Thanks, Penny. I have to say, for some reason, it's not completely condescending when you pat me on the head like that. I don't know if it's because I want the praise, or because I understand that you don't have any other way to express yourself to me." She glanced at Penny, who had a thoughtful look on her face. "We need to start language lessons soon. I like you too much to not be able to talk to you girl to girl."

Penny nodded, then after a second, patted her on the head again.

Mila laughed. "You're a bit of an asshole, Penny. I think I like that most about you. Now let's go help our handsome dwarf before he blows a gasket and charges in there to get the ring."

Penny bounced with laughter and puffed a smoke ring in agreement.

Mila grabbed a big cut of beef and peeled back the plastic, tossing the tray and wrapping in the garbage, then headed back over to Finn, who was still staring at the hound, trying to think of how to distract it. As soon as the hound smelled the approaching meat, it focused its burning-coal eyes on Mila and began to drool.

Mila held the steak out, close to the side of the cage, right above an opening designed to slide a bowl of food through. The hound turned and pressed its nose through one of the links in the fence, snorting at the smell of raw meat, and drooling even more.

"Can you get it now?" Mila asked.

Finn had a half-smile of wonderment on his face. "Damn good thinking. Give me a second."

He put his hand on the gate latch, now behind the hellhound, and took a deep breath. In one fluid motion, he opened the gate and grabbed hold of the ring, halfway down the hound's tail. The hound yipped and began to turn at the sudden attention, but Mila dropped the steak through the opening, and the animal dove down to the ground, snatching up the meat with a set of razor-sharp teeth and tore a chunk out.

Finn slammed the gate closed and took a deep breath. "Fuck, that thing is terrifying. Whoever thought of giving an apex predator stone skin was an asshole."

"Did you get it?" Mila asked, noting that the hound was still marble-skinned.

He held out the ring between a thick thumb and fore-finger. "Got it. It takes a second for the magic to wear off. There it goes."

She saw the white marble fur begin to lose its shine. At first, she thought the stone was becoming rough because the color never changed, but when the black and pink veins of the marble faded along with the shine, she realized that the hound just happened to have white fur to begin with.

She wondered if the marble coloring was a byproduct of the animal's original color, or if it was just a coincidence.

"She really is beautiful," Mila commented as they watched her devour the two pounds of meat in a few bites. "And really scary. Maybe she needs a little more to eat?"

"I'll get a couple of steaks for her," Finn said, pocketing the ring and walking toward the fridge. "Why don't you give Anita a call and give her the good news? And let her know that she'll need to come pick up her hound herself. We aren't doing a delivery on this one."

CHAPTER FOURTEEN

Finn dropped a couple more steaks on the ground and kicked them through the cage's opening for the hound. It was the third time he had fed the hound in the forty-five minutes they had been waiting for Anita and her people to arrive. The poor thing must have been starving. He felt a little bad that they had waited until this morning to come, instead of coming straight over the night before.

Mila and Penny were sitting on the cot, playing one of the games Mila had on her phone, Penny pointing out moves from her shoulder. It drove Finn nuts when she did that to him, but Mila didn't seem to mind, enjoying it as a group activity instead of thinking of Penny as backseat playing.

He leaned on the column in the middle of the cellar and watched them for a few minutes. Penny and Mila laughed at something on the screen, sharing a bond that was growing stronger as the days passed. He would feel jealous if he didn't feel the same way about Mila that Penny evidently did. There was something special about Mila, and it was driving Finn crazy that he couldn't tell what it was.

She had found the concealed door without even trying, which should have been nearly impossible for anyone who wasn't a powerful magic user. Even Penny had to have it pointed out to her, and she was practically made of magic. What did that say about Mila's potential?

"Hello? Finn? Mila? Are you down there?" Anita called down, the boards of the steps creaking as the black-haired elf slowly came down into the cellar.

Finn pushed off the column and turned to see Anita in a set of navy-blue overalls ducking under the low frame around the stairs. "Anita, good to see you." Finn stepped across the room to shake her hand.

She reeled back as he closed the distance quickly but smiled and took his hand in greeting. "You move pretty quietly for such a big man." She looked past him and saw Mila and Penny standing from the cot. "Dr. Winters, Penny. Good to see you again." She turned to the hound, who was finishing off her sixth hunk of meat, finally slowing down. "Oh, my poor baby," she crooned, showing more emotion than Finn had seen out of her yet. She knelt down beside the cage and reached a hand through a gap in the fencing.

"Oh, I wouldn't do that…" Finn started to warn her but stopped when he saw her petting the hound without any problem. In fact, the hound closed its eyes and pushed into the petting. "Oh, well, I suppose you know what you're doing."

A man in a blue jumpsuit like Anita's came down the stairs. "The truck is ready for transport, Anita." He gave

Finn a nod and went back up the stairs without further comment.

Mila let out a gasp, stepping up next to Finn. He spun to see Anita opening the latched gate and letting the hound out. Finn immediately had Fragar out, and he was impressed when he saw Mila had done the same with Gram. She had even gone so far as to whisper the power word, letting the golden blade unfurl to its full three-foot length.

"What are you doing?" Anita shouted, stepping between them and the hound whose hackles had stood as a low growl rumbled in its chest. "Are you insane? Put those things away, or she'll attack."

"That's what we're worried about!" Finn roared, crouching in a defensive position.

"She'll only attack you if she's provoked. Put the weapons up. Now!" Anita insisted, blocking the hound from seeing them.

Finn and Mila exchanged looks, and after a second, both spoke the power words to their weapons, letting them fold up into their handles. As soon as the blades were put away, the hound calmed down and nudged Anita's hand, wanting to be petted.

She let out a sigh of relief and scratched the hound's ear. "This hound is imprinted on me. That means she'll follow my orders, but only to a point. If she thinks I'm in danger, she'll attack."

"Well, that information would have been useful before you let her out of the cage," Finn said with a deep frown.

"I thought you knew that. Didn't we mention she was mine at the Menagerie?"

"Uh, no. That never came up." Finn rolled his eyes. "You were in such a hurry to get back to work, you forgot to mention that."

Anita seemed chagrined, but only a little. She pulled out a cigarette and lit it, blowing blue smoke into the air above her. "Well, sorry about that. I have to say, I'm kind of shocked that you were able to find this place so quickly. I figured it would take you three a few weeks at the least."

Finn saw Mila frowning at the smoking elf and looking over her shoulder toward the cot and table but decided not to comment on it. Instead, he turned to Anita.

"You can let your boss know that we did our part. We'll be over tomorrow to return the ring and talk about payment."

Anita shrugged. "I'll mention it if I happen to see him, but I doubt I will with taking care of this mess. He always seems to know what's going on anyway without anyone telling him. Come on, girl," she said, dropping her half-smoked cigarette on the ground and whistling while patting her leg.

The hound perked up and followed her out of the cellar.

Finn watched them go, then turned to Mila. "Okay, what did you just see that I missed?"

He knew she was thinking; her face was set in a half-frown, the face she always made when thinking something unpleasant.

Mila walked over and, with the hand not holding the sword, picked up the still-burning cigarette Anita had dropped and walked over to the small table. Finn followed and saw what had caught her attention.

She stubbed out the white filtered cigarette and raised an eyebrow when it was an exact match for the ones in the tray. "Something's fishy." Mila reached under her jacket and snapped Gram back into its holster before putting both hands on her hips. "Anita didn't seem all that surprised by what we found here. She didn't even mention that the hound had obviously already had its pups and that they're gone. And you saw the way she handled her, and just walked out of here with the hound following like it was no big deal. Did you notice the pawprints on the steps? Those animals were led out of here; they didn't break out and run away."

"I did notice that, but I don't know if that really implicates Anita." He crossed his arms, thinking it all through. "Peter steals the hounds…"

"With help," Mila interjected. "You saw the footage. He knew the parkway too well, and where to find the keys to that truck pretty quickly."

"Most likely had some inside help," Finn agreed. "The hound pups were born with stone skin because they happened to use the ring on the pregnant one. Preston seemed surprised by that, but Anita would have read the notes on the ring before using it, and I saw it mentioned in the ring's paperwork. Besides, they implied that it wasn't the first time they had used the ring on a hound during pregnancy." Finn pursed his lips in thought. "Okay, it's not looking good for Anita, but with enough research, anyone could have found out most of that stuff. I don't want to accuse her just because she's a little odd and abrasive. We can mention it to Preston when we see him tomorrow and see what he thinks."

"What about this?" Mila asked, pointing to the butts in the ashtray. "They're the exact same brand."

Finn gave a shrug. "Not proof, but something to keep in mind. Remember, this isn't a movie. Not everything means something. A lot of people buy the same brands of cigarettes. Could be coincidence."

Mila opened her mouth to argue but was distracted when her phone rang. She checked the caller ID, then answered. "Hey. You okay?" She mouthed "Danica" to Finn.

She listened for a few seconds before her eyes went wide.

"Are you serious? How many? Holy shit... Okay, we're on our way." She hung up the phone and slid it into her back pocket. "Danica said twelve gang members were brought into the hospital after they were attacked by wild dogs. They're in pretty bad shape. She also said the entire gang is made up of Selkies, whatever those are."

"Seal people," Finn said, turning for the stairs

Mila stayed close on his heels, Penny having to dig her claws into the leather of her jacket to stay upright.

"Seal people? How does that work?" She shook her head in confusion.

"Shir chees," Penny informed her unhelpfully.

Finn took pity on her and translated, "They're shapeshifters."

"Like werewolves?"

Mila hit the lights as they made their way out to the backyard. The late morning light was blinding after the relative dark of the cellar, but after a few blinks, Finn's eyes adjusted.

"Not exactly like werewolves. They are either seals or people, but it happens at will, not during a full moon."

"Well, regardless, Danica said for us to hurry before the police get there and keep us from talking to them."

Mila hit the unlock button on the Hellcat as they came out of the backyard from around the garage. She got in and started the car, but Finn stopped when he saw a black car parked on the street near where they had pulled into the dead-end road. Something about it caught his eye, and it took him a second to realize there was someone in the vehicle.

After a few seconds, the black car pulled into a driveway and turned around. It wasn't in any hurry, and they used their blinker to turn left and drive deeper into the old neighborhood, so they weren't trying to hide their intentions. He was wondering why the car had caught his eye in the first place when Mila rolled her window down and leaned over the center console.

"Come on. She said we only had twenty minutes or so to get there. What are you doing?"

Finn snapped out of it and climbed in. "Sorry. A car caught my eye. I don't think it was anything to worry about, though. Let's get out of here."

Penny hopped off Mila's shoulder and onto Finn's lap as Mila reversed out of the drive and sped down the street, taking a right toward the main road.

CHAPTER FIFTEEN

Mila parked on the second level of the hospital's attached garage so they could walk across the bridge directly into the emergency lobby. Finn followed, scanning the cars to see if he saw the black car from Peter's house, but there were too many to pick one out. Besides, they had come here directly, and he hadn't noticed the car following them.

Penny crawled down from his shoulder and settled into her hammock at the small of his back. He handed her the box of Charleston Chews after taking a few for himself. The sound of candies tumbling out of the box was at least muffled by his jacket.

"Danica said to tell the reception desk we're here to see her, and they'll page her over." Mila glanced back, seeing that he had dropped behind. "What are you looking for?"

Finn frowned and caught up with her. "I was looking for that car I saw. I don't know, something isn't sitting right with me."

"Is it here?" she asked, craning her neck to see back into the garage.

"I didn't see it, but there are a lot of cars here." He shrugged and continued across the bridge. "Come on, let's get in there."

They waited five minutes at the reception desk after the nurse paged Danica. Finn was amazed at the way Peabrains dealt with injuries. It all seemed so primitive compared to what magical healers could accomplish. He struggled to not hand out all the healing potions he had in his harness, but he knew it would throw the whole balance of the world out of sync. Wasn't that exactly what he was trying to prevent the Dark Star from doing in the first place?

Danica came down one of the halls. "Hey, guys." She waved for them to follow her, then led them through a set of doors into the main emergency ward. "I talked with the leader for a few minutes and knew you would want to hear about what happened. The cops are here taking a few statements, but I asked that Kevin, the leader, be saved for last. You probably have about five minutes until they get to him. Then he's going into surgery and will be out for a day or two."

"Why didn't they find a healer?" Finn asked. "I mean, as Selkies, they would be part of the magical community."

Danica sighed, stopping at a blue curtain and speaking softly. "Because most Magicals don't have the financial means to get hold of high-grade healing potions. At least here, they can get care and financial assistance through insurance. There isn't any insurance for magic. And if they come across some means for magical healing later down the line, then they can have their limbs grown back at that time. It's a harsh world we live in for those without the cash."

Finn frowned, not liking what he was hearing, but not unaccustomed to the way things worked. Even out in the universe as a whole, things still cost something.

Danica pulled back the curtain and let Mila and Finn through, closing it behind them. On the bed was a man who looked to be in his mid-twenties, with silky, brown hair and deep brown eyes. Knowing he was a shapeshifting seal made Finn think that his features were somewhat seal-like, but he didn't know if that was a projection of his knowledge, or if the guy really did look slightly seal-like.

"Kevin," Danica switched to the soft, but clear voice of a friendly doctor. "These are my friends I was telling you about. They're looking for the hellhounds and trying to get them off the street. Are you feeling up to talking to them?"

Kevin cleared his throat and tried to sit up in the bed a little more. That was when Finn noticed he was missing his left arm from the elbow down. The stump had been bandaged, but there was still a little blood seeping through. The young man looked pale, but he set his jaw and nodded.

"I'm Kevin Rivers," the Selkie said after clearing his throat again. His eyes widened a little at seeing Finn for the first time when Danica stepped to the side to check his readings on the machines beside the bed. "Are you a dwarf?"

Finn smiled and stepped closer. "I am. It's nice to meet you; you can call me Finn. This is my friend Mila. Could you tell us what happened here?"

The direct question pushed Kevin past his shock at

seeing a dwarf, and he nodded. "Yeah, my gang was having a meeting with another gang on our border."

"I'm sorry," Mila interrupted, "but you don't look like you're in a gang. Pardon me, but you look like a college student."

Finn agreed with her assessment. Finn had come across a lot of gang members in his and Penny's travels, and almost without exception, they had at least sported some tattoos or just had the rough look of people living a hard life. Kevin still had the fresh face of a middle-class kid, and he was their leader.

Kevin chuckled. " 'Gang' is not really the best word for it. It's just what we all call it when a group of like Magicals want to live and work together. We don't have traditional jobs, but we pool what resources we have and open businesses or ventures together."

"Ah, so it's a little like a commune or something," Mila guessed.

"A little, though that word has its own problems," Kevin said, grimacing and clutching at his bicep above the bandage.

"Are you in a lot of pain?" Danica asked, leaning in and checking the wrappings. "I can have them up your pain meds if you need me to."

He shook his head. "I'm fine, thanks, Doc." He gave her a smile before continuing. "Anyway, we were meeting with an Orc gang that borders us. They have a custom motorcycle shop and wanted to expand. We had just acquired a warehouse and were meeting with them to trade it for some land they have outside of town. Me and my people have a smokehouse restaurant, and we were looking to start farming our ingredients ourselves, you know how people love that farm-to-table stuff.

"Anyway, we all met in a neutral location near the warehouse. There were about a dozen of us from each group, and while Orcs aren't the friendliest people, we always got along pretty well. Things were going fine for the first ten minutes or so, when out of nowhere, about twenty hellhounds come charging out from behind the building. It was unlike anything I had ever seen! I mean, I've seen hellhounds at the Menagerie before, but out in the open like that, they were terrifying. And I swear this is true, even though it sounds nuts, but every one of them had stone skin."

"Actually," Finn reassured him, "I completely believe that part. It's one of the reasons we're trying to find them. What happened next?"

Kevin shook his head as the events played out in his head. "At first, it was chaos. We thought the orcs had decided to just take us out. Like I said, they're not the most upstanding people at the best of times... but then the hounds attacked them too. Blood was everywhere, scream-ing...it was horrible.

"After a second, the hounds stopped attacking the orcs, and they used the opportunity to run. But the things kept coming after me and my people. We did our best, but there was nothing we could do." Tears filled his eyes, and he held back a choking sob. "Three of my people were torn apart right in front of my eyes. We couldn't stop 'em at first, then one of my better offensive casters caught one with a ball of fire that blasted a chunk from it. Then just as fast as they had shown up, they ran off back the way they had come. I called 911, and they brought us here."

Mila gave him a sad smile and put a hand on his shoulder. "I'm so sorry."

He just nodded, wiping the tears from his eyes with his one good hand.

"Can you tell me the name of the motorcycle shop the orcs own?" Finn asked.

"Uh, yeah. It's called Colorado Bobber Company. They're near the 470 and 85 interchange, in the warehouses over there."

Finn had a thought. "Do you know who the Dark Star is?"

Kevin stared at him, then looked around to see if anyone was listening, which was pointless since the walls were made of cloth. He frowned and said in a whisper, "Everyone knows about her. The idea of a magical nation sounds great and all, but we don't approve of her methods to get it. A lot of Magicals do, though, and don't care how bloody the war would be if they could have their own nation when it was all over. The orcs are eager to get on her good side; they talk about it openly with other gangs."

"Thanks, Kevin." Finn gave him a half-smile. "You've been a big help. When you're feeling better, come to the market under the LODO district, and ask for Remmy the goblin. She'll be able to find me. Maybe I can help you and your people out a little in exchange for some help from you."

He nodded. "Thanks, I will."

The curtain was pulled back, and two officers stood next to a nurse with a surprised look on her face.

"You can't be in here!" the nurse said before seeing Danica step around Finn. "Oh, Dr. Meadows. I didn't realize you were here."

"It's okay, we were just leaving." Danica turned to Kevin. "I'll talk to you after your surgery. Probably in the morning, okay?"

He smiled at her, then winced in pain.

Danica led Finn and Mila out of the curtained-off room as the cops stepped in and began taking Kevin's statement. "I need to get back to my floor. Will you two be okay getting out of here?" she asked when they were back out in the hall.

"We'll be fine," Mila said, giving Danica a tight hug. "See you at home."

"Okay." She skipped backward a few steps while waving goodbye. "See ya." She turned and disappeared around a corner.

Mila turned and gave Finn a frown. "What was that about the Dark Star? You think she has something to do with all this?"

They started making their way back out to the bridge to the parking garage, passing through the waiting area.

"I think she might be part of everything," He half-joked. "It seems like every time we find something out, there are more questions. But the one question that keeps coming back to me is who has the hounds. I know that sounds dumb, it's kind of the point of our job here. But I'm just thinking, who gains the most out of having a pack of hellhounds? Obviously, Peter was hired to steal the hounds for someone in particular, he never intended on taking the hounds then finding a buyer on the open market, that much is obvious from the texts on his phone with J. But what does this J have to gain from attacking a random group of people?"

"Not just a random group," Mila pointed out as they stepped into the afternoon sun, squinting her eyes against the sudden change in light level. "A group of Magicals. From what I'm gathering, it's rare to find large groups of Magicals out in the open without at least some nonmagicals around."

Finn nodded. "That's a really good point. But why care who you attack?"

Mila shrugged. "Probably because nonmagicals would freak out and tell everyone about the giant, stone-skinned, red-eyed dogs. But Magicals are used to keeping quiet when it comes to matters magical."

"So, this was a test. A trial run. Maybe they needed to know how much control they had over the hounds." Finn grinned as it all started to make sense. "Remember Kevin said the hounds attacked all of them at first, but then switched to only attacking his people? It sounds like someone was trying to control them and needed to know the limitations. It sounds like they haven't bonded with the hounds but are using some sort of device to control them."

Mila hit the fob for the Hellcat, and the headlights flashed as the doors unlocked. They were still an aisle over from the car, but she pressed the remote start, and it roared to life as they approached.

A car turned the corner, the tires squealing on the smooth concrete, making Finn spin and pull out Fragar automatically. He caught Mila doing the same out of the corner of his eye. The vehicle was a minivan, and it turned sharply into a spot, and a man jumped out of the driver's door, not paying any attention to them, and pulled open the back door of the van. He picked up a little girl in a bicycle helmet who was crying and holding her arm.

Finn relaxed when the man ran across the bridge to the emergency room. He turned back to Mila, and stepped toward the car, right out of the path of a fast-moving bubble the size of his fist.

Time slowed down as he watched the bubble that had just missed him fly directly at Mila, her eyes growing wide at the incoming attack. He tried to run toward her, but the bubble exploded on her chest before he had taken a single step.

She let out a scream of pain and was blown over the hood of the car behind her in a tumbling roll.

CHAPTER SIXTEEN

"Penny, help Mila!" Finn roared, spinning to find the attacker.

Penny shot out from under his jacket, her wings flapping hard.

Finn whispered Fragar's power word, unfolding the axe just in time to bat away a second fast-moving bubble. He spotted the caster charging from between two cars, his hands up and flowing with golden light as another bubble formed and shot out at Finn.

The attacker was concealed behind a black mask that covered the bottom half of his face and a hooded black shirt over black tactical pants. He reminded Finn of an assassin from a modern-day ninja movie.

Finn crouched before springing forward and to the side, dodging the third attack and closing the distance between them. He could feel the rage bubbling in his blood, and let it flow freely, giving himself an extra burst of speed as his vision went red at the edges.

The assassin formed a fourth bubble, dodging Finn's

charge, and let the attack fly at point-blank range, hitting Finn full in the chest, as he countered the assassin's feint and came right at him.

The bubble exploded, ripping a hole in Finn's shirt and tearing at his flesh, but he barely felt it in the berserker's rage. He could feel the spittle flying from his mouth as he roared at the man in black, and swung Fragar, two-handed, at his head.

A clanging of metal rang out in the parking garage as the assassin got a two-foot blade up just in time to stop the axe before it scalped him. Finn had far more weight behind his weapon, though, and forced his way closer, making the man roll away to get some distance between them.

Finn didn't even bother running after the man, he just bunched up his legs, and leaped across the distance, Fragar once again coming after him in a two-handed swing. This time, when the short sword met with the glowing axe, a large chip of the sword's blade whizzed off to ricochet off a concrete column.

Again, the assassin had to roll back. This time, he was forming a magical attack before he was even back on his feet. A tight cluster of bubbles exploded out like a shotgun, making Finn roll to the side. The grouping of magical projectiles zipped across the garage and rocked a car, blasting holes in its steel fender.

"*Gunna salainn!*" Finn shouted, coming up on one knee.

A blast of rock salt shot from his hand and ripped into the assassin's leg, spraying blood, and knocking him to the ground. Finn took his chance and leaped across the gap, swinging his axe down. It sparked, gouging a huge chunk from the smooth tarmac where the man had just rolled away.

Finn kicked out to the side, catching the attacker in the ribs as he rolled to his feet, eliciting a grunt and a satisfying crack of at least one rib.

They stared at one another, the attacker realizing he had miscalculated his target's abilities, and Finn wondering if he should just throw Fragar at him.

The attacker held up a hand, snapping a large bubble around himself.

Finn growled and, sprinting forward, reached out for the assassin. He got his hand around something hard and pulled back with all his might. Just as his hand and whatever he held was outside of the forming bubble, the whole thing popped, and the attacker was gone.

The rage was flowing fully through his blood, but the thought of Mila being hurt, and needing his help, forced his berserker's desire to kill the enemy into submission and let his rational thinking start to come to the fore.

He stood breathing deep and ragged breaths for a minute until he was able to blink back the red haze from his eyes. Then he looked over to where Mila had been and saw her booted feet sticking out beyond the front bumper of the car beside the Hellcat. Running to her, Finn slid around the front of the car on his knees, ignoring the sting of concrete ripping through his jeans. He stopped himself from moving closer when he saw her sitting up with an empty healing potion in her hand.

"Fuck me, I thought you were dead," he finally said through deep breaths.

"I was fine. I got the mithril armor up just in time. It

hurt like a son of a bitch, but I was fine." She hiked a thumb at Penny, who was glaring at her from her shoulder. "She made me drink this just to be sure."

"Squee! Shi shirir, chi shi!" Penny insisted, smoke pouring out of her in her anger.

Mila just stared at the tirade, not commenting or needing translation. She turned back to Finn. "Are you okay?"

He nodded. "Yeah, but the guy got away. Got this off him before he teleported, though." He held up a pocket torn off the assassin's pants.

"A piece of cloth?"

"Better." He pulled a phone from the cloth. "Hopefully we can get into it and see who's after us." He looked around and checked that the garage was still clear, then held out a hand to Mila. "Come on, we should probably get out of here in case anyone saw us."

She took his hand, and he helped her to her feet.

"You okay to drive?" he asked as she wobbled a little.

"Yeah, just a little rush of blood to the head. Let's go."

Two minutes later, Mila's car squealed out of the parking garage and onto the main street. She changed lanes and hit the gas to get through a yellow light.

Finn pulled out the assassin's phone and hit the power button. To his surprise, the phone had no security on it whatsoever and opened to the home page.

"I would have thought an assassin would have better security." Finn showed the open phone to Mila, who glanced away from the road just long enough to see.

"I don't think that's his personal phone. It looks like a

burner." She changed lanes and slowed for the next light. "See how there's only the one app besides the defaults? I don't know anyone who doesn't have at least one game on their phone. What is that app anyway? The one at the bottom right."

Finn didn't recognize the icon, but then, he didn't recognize any of them; he only opened his phone when he needed to know the time. He held the phone down for Penny to take a look at.

She settled into his lap and took the phone with an eye roll. She punched the app with a talon, and it opened into an extremely basic messaging platform.

"It looks like a text conversation," Finn explained as Mila tapped her finger on the steering wheel. "It's from an unsaved number, asking the assassin to complete a contract. They agree on a price, and then...oh shit."

"What?" Mila gunned it, barking the tires a little on takeoff as the light turned green.

"It's a picture of you and me at the hospital. It looks like surveillance footage from the hospital's security cameras. It was when we were walking down that hall to the morgue with Danica, but she's been cropped out."

Mila frowned, but didn't say anything, just continued driving and tapping her finger on the wheel.

After a second, Finn glanced at her silence.

"What's wrong?"

"How much did they say the contract was worth?" she asked.

He checked back through the messages. "A hundred grand each."

She snorted with laughter. "Obviously, they had no idea

how hard we were going to be to kill. I would have asked for at least a million apiece."

He chuckled at her joke but saw it for what it was, a deflection.

"Look. They're going to try again, but they know we'll be on our guard for a while. This isn't the first time I've had a price on my head. Technically, I think there still is one from the Priestesses of Granth, but I can't remember if it had a time limit or not. Regardless, I think you need to keep your mithril on at all times while we're out. I don't want a lucky shot taking you out."

"I thought assassins went for headshots," she said drolly.

He waved off the comment. "Nah, that's only in the movies. A body shot is much easier and just as effective in most cases. Once you're down, that's when they take the headshot, just to be sure."

"That's not really filling me with confidence." She smiled at him. "Have I ever told you you're shit at motivational speeches?"

"You've mentioned it." He smiled along with her, then looked around, trying to figure out where they were. "Where are you taking us, anyway?"

"To the orcs' motorcycle shop. Figured it was the next logical step." She flipped on her blinker and turned onto the 470 East entrance ramp.

He nodded. "Good thinking."

She snorted, then mumbled, "Whatever we find, it can't be worse than an exploding magical bubble to the chest."

Mila turned down a side street into an older section of warehouses. The corrugated steel of many of the buildings had copious amounts of rust coming through the old paint, along with rusted stairs and scaffolding attached at slightly leaning angles, now that the buildings had settled over the years.

Despite the run-down quality of the buildings, it was obvious that the warehouses were still in use as the occasional truck backed into a loading dock, or a small group of workers smoked in a tight cluster against the chill of late autumn.

Finn scanned the area as they moved to the second row of warehouses, following the directions given by the GPS on Mila's phone. It seemed like an odd place for a business that served customers, but maybe the custom motorcycle market was more willing to go to sketchy places to get the proper work done.

"There it is." Mila pointed to a warehouse down the street. "It's nicer than I thought it would be."

Finn agreed. The corrugated siding had been painted a deep royal blue, with a red sign above the middle of the medium-sized building featuring a large 'CBC' drawn in a way that made it look like a bobber motorcycle.

They turned down the street and drove slowly.

"Huh, they have a parking lot. Must have torn down the building next to them or something," Finn observed, looking at the way the buildings around them were packed in one next to the other. "I say just park in there but keep to the back of the lot."

"Don't we want to be close to the door, just in case this goes sideways?" Mila asked, pulling into the lot and slowly rumbling toward the back.

"No." Finn and Penny shared a look, Penny giving a slight nod. "Look, I need you to stay in the car and keep an eye out."

Mila frowned and stopped the car to look at him. There weren't many other cars in the lot, so they stood out like a sore thumb. "I can be helpful inside. People like to see a pretty face when they're getting grilled for info."

"True, but these aren't the kind of people you're used to. These are Orcs. They think things like sharpened teeth and spiked clubs are sexy. You're not their type." He pointed to a spot that was closer to the main building but against the back fence. "Park there. I have a feeling this is going to go one of two ways. Either there's going to be an all-out fight, or I'm not going to get any information, but my questions will make them nervous, and one of them might make a run for it. We need eyes outside."

Finn didn't exactly believe they needed a lookout, but after the attack in the garage, and Mila coming so close to death, he didn't want to put her in danger again. Most Orcs were aggressive, but they weren't as dumb as people assumed. If a fight broke out, he would rather not have to look out for Mila while he was going hog wild.

Mila stared at him for a second but finally gave in. "Fine. I'll go through the two phones and see if there's anything of interest that we missed."

She backed into the spot so she'd have a clear view of the main entrance and the back of the building at the same time and shut the car off.

"Thanks." He patted her knee, then climbed out of the car, trying to ignore her disappointed looks.

Penny climbed up onto his shoulder and looked back at the car as she and Finn headed for the blue painted steel steps that led to the front door. "Chi she shi?"

Finn shrugged, making the dragon have to grab onto his collar to stay balanced. "She's probably mad, but it'll be better this way. I'm still pretty shaken up that she took a blast right to the chest. I thought for sure she was dead."

Penny nodded, her face serious. It had obviously shaken her up as well.

They climbed the steps, and Finn took a second to look through the window in the top half of the steel door. He didn't see anyone inside, but there was a small reception desk and a few chairs for waiting customers, along with a surprisingly healthy potted plant in the corner.

"Looks like a legit business. Let's hope they at least hear me out before one of them throws a punch."

He sucked in a breath and pulled the door open. To his relief, there was no door chime, letting them enter without being heard.

He wasn't exactly sure what to expect with this gang. Traditionally, Orcs and dwarves got along even worse than trolls and dwarves, who were in the midst of a multi-thousand-year war. He was hoping the fact that the orcs on *Earth* had not seen a dwarf in over a thousand years would put a damper on their snap judgment, but he made sure Fragar was loose in its holster just in case.

The waiting room was fairly small, and he saw that there was a pod coffee maker in the corner with a nice selection of coffees in a metal rack. There was a doorbell button built into the reception desk with a note that said *Ring for service*, but he ignored it, heading instead to the door behind the desk that led to the shop.

He took a look through the window in the door, seeing at least a dozen orcs sitting in a circle around a half-constructed motorcycle. They sat on seats ranging from rolling chairs to milk crates, and it looked like they were halfway through lunch, most of them holding half a foot-long from Subway in their dirty hands. He could hear laughter and loud voices.

Each of the orcs had a low-level concealment spell over them, but it wasn't strong enough to keep him from seeing their true forms underneath. Their natural skin was just a greener version of what the concealment spell showed as every color from pale white to dark brown, but the tattoos that covered their arms and necks were real enough. He didn't recognize most of the symbols, but he had to assume that at least a few of them were unwholesome in one way or another. Unlike trolls, who had long, pointed noses and wide-set mouths, orcs looked relatively human except for the small tusks that jutted from their lower jaws. They all had hair and wide, normal-shaped noses. But like trolls, they were tall, at least as tall as Finn. Most of them even had an inch or two on his six-five.

They all wore jeans, t-shirts, and black leather covered in grease spots from engine work, but the designs on the t-shirts were all over the place. Some were old rock band logos, while others featured American eagles holding guns or flags. One even had a My Little Pony character in a lewd pose with rainbows shooting from its butt.

A lot of the orcs had bandages on their limbs, with spots of blood coming through from fresh wounds. Finn guessed that was the work of the hounds.

As he reached for the door handle, Penny tapped his cheek and pointed to the far corner of the shop. Finn squinted, trying to pick out what she had seen, but all he could see were racks of parts and machinery, along with rows of motorcycles. He was about to ask what she was pointing at when he saw them.

Behind a tall rack filled with tires were two people standing close and talking. The taller of the two was an orc, but the other wore a long jacket with a hood up, concealing his face. He was larger than the normal Peabrain, and the length of his arms said he was either another orc or a troll, but the rack of tires was concealing too much of him for Finn to tell which.

"Good catch," he praised Penny. "See if you can keep an eye on the one in the hood." Finn set his jaw and walked through the door.

As soon as the door opened, the entire group turned his way. One of the orcs in an AC/DC t-shirt broke away and jogged over as Finn walked down a small set of steps to the shop's ground level.

"Hey, sorry, we're closed for lunch. You can come back in half an hour," he said, a smile on his face.

As soon as the orc got a good look at Finn, and Penny on his shoulder, his smile dropped, and he stopped a few paces away.

"Who the fuck are you?" His light, friendly manner had vanished.

Finn gave a bright smile. "Hey, guys. I'm Finnegan Dragonbender, but you all can call me Finn. I just had a few questions about what happened with you and the Selkies today."

"You a cop or something?" the one in the pony shirt asked, nearly spitting when he said "cop."

"No," a deep voice from behind the group rumbled. "He's a fucking dwarf."

The figure came around the group, and Finn could see it was the orc that had been talking to the hooded figure, which was now nowhere to be seen. This orc was obviously in charge and stood a good head taller than Finn. He wore a leather jacket covered in silver zippers and studs.

"My race really has nothing to do with it. I'm looking for information on the hellhounds that attacked you earlier, that's all." Finn held out his hands to show he had no intention of attacking.

"I've heard about you, dwarf." The leader sneered down at Finn as he stepped close, his hands in his jacket pockets. "Newcomer making waves and throwing money around like it fucking grows on trees. Word is you're in bed with that fucking cow, Meriwether."

"I'm doing a job for him, but I wouldn't say we're in bed together. The guy hasn't even bought me dinner yet." Finn gave a half-smile. "You seem to know a lot about me. Can't say I have the pleasure of knowing you." He held out a hand to the orc. "The name's Finn. And you are?"

The orc slowly looked down at his offered hand, then back up at his face. "Not interested in helping you. I suggest you get the fuck out of here before you outstay your welcome."

At that, the rest of the orcs put their lunches down and stood up, flexing hands and necks in a show of strength.

Finn slowly put his hand down. "Okay. What's it going to take to get a little info? Just trying to keep the hounds off the street, not trying to bust your balls or anything. People are getting hurt, and it's only going to get worse. I already know that the hounds attacked you." He pointed to an orc with his forearm wrapped in bandages. "I also know that they stopped attacking you after the initial swarm. I just need to know if you saw anything out of the ordinary after the attack. Maybe where the hounds went? Who was giving them orders? Anything would help."

The leader stepped close enough for Finn to smell his musky body odor and hot breath. "Are you fucking deaf? We don't have anything to talk to you about. You're just like my great pa told me you people are— stubborn and entitled. I can't wait to get the fuck out of here and finally have a place where we don't have to put up with your fucking kind."

Finn frowned in confusion. "My kind? I'm pretty sure I'm the only one left. Do you mean people who follow the law? People who care about others? I'm confused."

The leader ground his teeth, his tusks moving from side to side as he glared at Finn, but he didn't say anything.

Finn knew they weren't going to volunteer anything, but that didn't mean he couldn't get something out of them. He had a feeling they knew who the dogs belonged to, or at least had a good idea. He decided to try something that didn't usually work for him. He was going to bluff.

"Look." He gave them all a winning smile, holding up his hands, and using a reasonable voice. "I can appreciate you guys wanting to keep to yourselves, but my boss isn't the kind to suffer fools lightly. She wants the hounds, and she sent me to find them. If you help me out, I can put in a good word for you. I hear you want to get in the organization, right? Well, here's your chance."

The leader frowned, looking him up and down, then raised an eye ridge. "You're telling me you work for the Dark Star?"

Finn gave him a "you said it, not me" shrug, but nodded.

The key to bluffing was to only lie about the small things, and let your opponent assume the rest. Finn usually wasn't very good at that, but he had bluffed his way out of a few situations over the years, and it seemed the orcs here on *Earth* were just as dense as the ones everywhere else.

The orc smiled, showing a row of yellow teeth behind his tusks. "That's interesting, considering I just talked to her contact a few minutes ago, and he told me she was sorry that *her* hounds had attacked my men. Said they were testing out the capabilities of their control, and it got away from them. Even gave me some compensation." He pulled out an envelope stuffed with cash and waved it in Finn's face before stuffing it back into his pocket. "We got a job if we want it, too."

Finn kept his smile on the outside, but inside, he cursed.

The orcs on *Earth* were brighter or luckier than he was used to. Probably luckier, considering the one in the My Little Pony shirt had one finger a good knuckle-and-a-half deep in his nose. It looked like he was trying to scratch his brain and succeeding.

Finn took the exchange as a win, though. Even if his bluff didn't work, he'd gotten the info he was after: the Dark Star was behind this.

Now he just needed to figure out what she was planning to do with the hounds.

He sniffed indignantly. "How do you know he worked for the Dark Star? He could have just been some guy trying to cover his tracks."

The leader laughed, looking at his men, who started laughing along with him. Finn decided he should probably stay on their good side, so he started laughing too.

That was when the leader slammed his fist into Finn's face so hard that Finn saw stars and ended up on his ass. Penny fluttered up into the air and looked down at him, waiting for the signal.

Finn wiped blood from his nose and mustache, looking at the bright red smeared across the back of his hand. "That wasn't very nice."

"It wasn't supposed to be, asshole." The leader laughed down at him.

Finn smiled up at him, blood on his teeth. "And here I thought this was going to be a friendly chat."

"Fuck friendly chats. I leave that shit to Oprah."

Finn frowned. "Damn, dude. That was a hell of a comeback. It's not as good as mine's going to be, though."

The orc stepped over Finn and leaned down, his face full of murder. "Oh yeah? And what eloquent comeback do you have for me, little man?"

Finn's eyes turned snowy gray, and he smiled.

"*Gunna salainn.*"

CHAPTER EIGHTEEN

Mila watched Finn peek through the window at the front entrance before opening the door and slipping inside.

"Be careful, you two," she whispered to herself, picking up the phone Finn had taken from the assassin, and hitting the power button.

She subconsciously rubbed her chest where the assassin's magic had blasted her, sending her ass over teakettle. The hit had hurt like a son of a bitch, and she knew it would have left a hell of a bruise, even with the mithril chainmail protecting her from harm, if Penny hadn't forced the healing potion down her throat.

If she had been honest with Finn, she would have told him that it had scared the shit out of her. She had spoken her power word for the armor only a fraction of a second before the magic hit her, and only then because Finn had seemed so sure they were going to be attacked. He had some sixth sense when it came to people trying to kill him, and she was a little jealous of that. Whenever she was alone, she felt like she was vulnerable, even though she had always been okay in the past.

However, the past hadn't involved a secret world of magic. Then again, her lifelong connection with insects wasn't exactly normal. Maybe she had some magic in her family, like a great-uncle who was a wizard or something.

She chuckled at the thought of Harry being her long-lost relative, then pursed her lips, remembering something that she, Danica, and Finn had talked about a few weeks before.

They had told her the history of the people on *Earth*, as well as they knew it. Finn informed her that *Earth* was a giant spaceship that had gotten lost. He had a lot of details about what was on it, what it was for, etc. But while that was interesting, it was kind of irrelevant to her current situation. At this point, *Earth* was a planet, and it wasn't going anywhere, so aside from understanding that natural disasters were mostly just ship malfunctions, and what and who the Huldu were, she didn't really care all that much.

What Danica had to say was a lot more informative to Mila's particular place in the world. She'd told her about how thousands of years ago, for some unknown reason, the Peabrains had all forgotten about magic, and their collective magical brain had gone to sleep.

As an anthropologist, the idea of an entire civilization forgetting about magic fascinated her. How could such an event happen? Was it a choice? An accident? No one knew the truth. But they did know that, sometimes, on a rare occasion, a Peabrain would "wake up," suddenly able to touch and control their magic.

Mila hoped that she was one of the lucky ones. She loved fantasy stories, and if she were to become a magic user, it would be a literal dream come true. The idea that she could one day do the things she'd seen Magicals do was one of the reasons she'd decided to take a year off from work and focus on helping Finn and Penny.

Well, it was one of the reasons, anyway.

Mila blinked and shook her head, coming out of her thoughtful state. She noticed that the phone she was holding had timed out and the screen had gone blank again.

"Come on, Mila, you're the lookout," she scolded herself. "Stop daydreaming."

She rolled her eyes and glanced at the building, scanning to see if anything had changed. Everything looked the same, so she reactivated the assassin's phone.

Now that she had a chance to look at it while not driving, she saw that there had actually been two apps installed. The messaging app didn't show any new notifications when she checked, so she moved on to the second app.

Its icon was a little cartoon ghost with crossbones behind it, a little like a pirate flag. She expected some kind of game, but when she loaded it up, it was a fairly crude message board. It looked like a primitive Wikipedia, but after reading the titles of the threads, she realized it was much darker than its little icon had led her to believe. It was a job site for people of questionable intent. There were listings like, "need wife taken out," and "business partner's insurance yours for action."

She scrolled through and was shocked there were so

many people who not only knew how to get to the site but were using it. There were thousands of requests for hitmen and thieves and even calls to join terrorist organizations.

The site made her skin crawl, and she closed the app with a shaking finger.

When this was all over, she was going to have to give the phone to the police, or maybe the FBI.

She opened the other app again and read through the messages about her and Finn's assassination contract. The content was exactly what Finn had said it was, but just before closing the app, she noticed that the user's name doing the hiring was K. She couldn't find any number associated with the username, but she pulled out Peter's phone and scrolled through the contacts. Sure enough, K was one of the four saved.

The sound of a steel door opening made her look up. The front door at the side of the building was clear, and she frowned until movement caught her eye, and she glanced over to see a large, hooded figure in a long coat coming out from a shipping dock at the back of the building.

She scrunched down a little in her seat so she wouldn't be spotted, but not so low that she couldn't watch him.

He was big, maybe even Finn's size, but with very long arms, almost like an ape. A long, dark brown, hooded trench coat covered him completely, and a pair of black leather gloves with the fingers cut out concealed everything but his fingertips, but she was too far away to see if the fingers were human or orcish. The man pulled out a phone and scrolled through it for a second before putting it to his ear, then started walking toward a sedan parked against the building, right in front and to the left of where Mila sat in the Hellcat.

The man kept looking over his shoulder and was talking animatedly into the phone. His big, sweeping gestures reminded her of someone, but she drove the thought from her mind, not wanting to get distracted the way she had earlier.

Mila frowned, not sure what to do. Ideally, she would like to follow this guy. He was obviously upset that Finn was inside since he had come out soon after Finn went in, but she couldn't leave without Finn. Besides, her black Hellcat wasn't the most inconspicuous car to follow someone in; the rumbling engine alone would get her noticed.

She glanced down at the two phones in her hands, and an idea came to her.

The battery on the assassin's phone was nearly full compared to Peter's, which only had a twenty percent charge. She chose the assassin's phone and pulled up the app store, quickly typing what she was looking for in the search bar. She hit the download button, then did the same for her own phone. Luckily, the warehouse was located close to a cell tower that didn't see much use, so the app downloaded and installed quickly.

Glancing over the steering wheel, she saw that the figure was standing beside his driver's side door, looking through his pockets for keys with one hand while holding the phone with the other.

Her phone dinged, and she immediately opened the app

on both phones, pairing them with each other. It took a few seconds, punctuated by her mumbling for them to hurry. After what felt like an eternity, both phones dinged. She dropped hers on the passenger seat and opened the glove box, pulling out a roll of duct tape, mentally thanking Finn for making her keep some in the car just in case they needed to tie anyone up.

She ripped off a strip about a foot long and stuck it to the phone's back, so there were a good four inches hanging off each side.

She opened her door as quietly as she could, watching to see if the man had heard her, but he was just then hitting the unlock button on his keys. She was behind him slightly, and off to the side, so she took a chance and timed her dash to when he opened his door and turned to get in.

She moved as quickly and quietly as she could, but every crunch of stone, every footfall, sounded like a marching band to her ears.

The man didn't seem to notice her crouching and running behind his car, due to him shouting something she didn't quite catch in her focused state.

She slid to a stop just as he slammed his door shut, and she flopped onto her back, quickly trying to tape the phone to the underside of the bumper, but what could have been years of road dust was making the job all but impossible.

The car roared to life, and she saw the reverse lights come on above her. She was still trying to clean the road dust off the car's undercarriage so the tape would stick better when the car started to roll backward.

Her heart stopped as she saw herself getting backed

over while trying to tape a phone to a car, but luckily, the man abruptly stepped on the brakes.

Mila could hear the man shouting into the phone as she quickly pressed the tape to the now relatively clean underside of the bumper, and the vehicle began rolling back once again.

Tucking her arms in, Mila rolled to the side as fast as she could. She let out a yelp as the car backed over her hair and pinned her to the ground for a second. She could feel the tire continue to move, raking against her shoulders, and she whispered the power word for her armor just as the tire began to gather up the leather at the back of her jacket. The leather, now being sandwiched between the ground and the inexorable rolling rubber, was starting to tighten around her midsection. A cool, flowing feeling that accompanied her armor forming from out of her skin made her nearly gasp in relief as it took most of the building pressure from her ribs.

The sound of ripping leather, accompanied by a sudden release of pressure, let her finally roll completely out of the way. She continued rolling until she was behind the car parked next to the sedan, then tucked herself up under the rear end so she wouldn't be seen by the large man as he drove away.

She calmed her breathing when she heard the car's engine rev and then the tires barking as he took off with a heavy foot. A few stones were kicked up and hit her in the head and shoulders, but she kept her mouth closed just in case he could hear her cry out in pain.

She waited until she couldn't hear anything but the

normal background noise of traffic on the freeway a block or two away before she rolled out from under the car and up on one knee, checking that he was gone, and not just sitting at the other end of the parking lot. She sighed with relief when she saw the coast was clear.

The thought of someone inside seeing her suddenly became her number one concern, and she glanced around to be sure no one else had come out, then sprinted to her car and jumped in.

Her heart was beating at twice its normal rate, but she felt giddy about what she had just done.

She patted herself down, checking that she was still in one piece, and found several pieces of gravel and twigs in her hair, as well as a sore spot where a large section of it had been pulled away when the car rolled over her, but she was otherwise unharmed.

Her jacket, on the other hand, had been torn all the way from armpit to hem, the leather white and stretched around the rip.

"Fuck. I really liked this jacket."

She quickly felt around the back of her corset that Gram and the one remaining healing potion were intact. Once again, she breathed a sigh of relief when she felt both items tucked securely in their places.

She had to admit that the corset made a pretty good utility belt, and it was obviously more durable than her jacket.

She pulled the jacket off and tossed it into the backseat, looking up just in time to see the front door of the motorcycle shop get blown off its hinges by the flying body of an orc.

The orc was wearing a t-shirt with a pony shitting out a rainbow, which Mila though was an odd detail for her to pick up on, considering the situation.

She started the Hellcat with a rumbling roar and threw it into drive, figuring Finn would be out soon. She was right, but not in the manner she had anticipated.

He came flying out the door horizontally, over the railing, landing on the orc with the pony shirt. When he rolled to his feet, he sprinted her way at full speed. There was blood all over his face, and he had a swollen eye; she was slightly satisfied to see that his jacket was pretty torn up as well.

She hit the gas and met him halfway across the distance, sliding to a stop as he pulled the door open, but he didn't get in.

"What are you doing? Get in here!" Mila shouted.

She quickly realized what the problem was.

"Where's Penny?"

"Right on my heels, but she wanted a little security that they couldn't follow us." His voice was tight with worry.

A flame bigger than any she had ever seen from the tiny dragon shot out of the front door, followed by another, then Penny's sleek body came shooting out of the smoke and flame like the *Millennium Falcon* at the end of *Return of the Jedi*.

Mila shouted her approval much as Chewy had.

Finn jumped in the car but kept the door open. "Let's get the hell out of here."

Mila stepped on the gas, letting all seven hundred horses loose, and spun the tires before the traction control kicked in, and they rocketed across the lot.

Penny shot through Finn's open door, splaying her wings to stop her momentum, filling the car with the smell of smoke. Finn pulled the door closed behind her, and Mila turned onto the road, the car sliding sideways before straightening out and chewing up the distance like it hadn't been fed in years.

Mila looked in the rearview mirror and saw smoke coming from the back of the shrinking building.

"Did you set the place on fire?" she asked, her eyes wide.

"No, of course not," Finn said like she was crazy. Then he looked down at Penny, who was guiltily not looking at either of them. "We didn't, right?"

Penny crossed her arms and gave a shrug. "Sir chich."

Finn pressed his lips together, looking down at the little dragon for a few seconds. He then looked at Mila. "Turns out we did, but it was only a little one."

"How little?" Mila asked though she wasn't sure she wanted to know.

That had been a legitimate business, after all.

"Well, she *said* it was little, but she is a fire-breathing dragon, so 'little' to her is...questionable."

Penny turned on him, her eyes narrowed. She started squeaking and pointing her talon at him, shaking it like a mother scolding her child. Her tirade included several bursts of flame and smoke, making Mila roll the windows down so she could see where she was going.

Finn held up his hands in surrender. "Okay, I get it. You did the right thing."

Penny narrowed her eyes and pointed at Mila. "Squee."

Finn frowned, then turned to Mila. "She wants me to

tell you that we could have used your help in there. Sorry for not taking you with us."

Mila looked at the blood streaming over his face and matting in his beard. She had never seen him quite this beat-up. "How many of them were there?"

"About a dozen or so." He shrugged, finding some napkins in the glove box under the roll of tape. He began to wipe up the blood but ended up just pressing the wad to his face and leaning back. "Well, at first, there were a dozen. I probably could have handled them, but they had another ten or twenty in the back room that came running when the fight started."

Mila balked at the number. "You were fighting thirty orcs, and you think I should have come in with you? Are you insane?"

"Chi squee shir." Penny folded her arms and tapped her foot.

Finn chuckled, then groaned when his nose smacked into his hand as Mila hit a bump turning onto the main road. "She said that if you were there, the orcs might not have attacked since you're a better talker than me. For the record, I would like to say that she was against you coming when we were walking in."

"Well, it doesn't matter," Mila said excitedly. "I think I got us a lead while you were getting your ass kicked."

"Hey! I did *not* get my ass kicked. I was overwhelmed and sucker-punched. Tell the ten guys who won't be able to eat without straws how they kicked my ass, and they'll call you a liar," Finn said defensively.

"Well, then I think I got us a lead while *you* were

kicking ass," Mila amended. "Did you see a guy in a hooded trench coat in there?"

"Yeah, I think he works for the Dark Star. Why? What did you do?" Finn gave her a sidelong glance, an effect that was ruined by the bloody napkin pressed to his face.

She gave him a shit-eating grin. "I put a tracker on his car."

CHAPTER NINETEEN

"Where did you get a tracker?" Finn was having a hard time focusing due to the throbbing in his nose, and the burning of at least one broken rib if he breathed in too deep.

Mila handed her phone to Penny after opening it with her thumbprint. "See the new app at the bottom? Open it up."

Penny complied, holding the phone so that both she and Finn could see it. "Phone Finder" was splayed across the screen. When the app fully opened, they could see the device name of the assassin's phone listed.

"That's the one. Select it," Mila instructed, pulling into a gas station after checking that they weren't being followed by a pissed off motorcycle gang.

Penny hit the button, and the app showed a map with a red dot moving along 85, back into town.

"Chi?"

"I paired it with the assassin's phone so I could track it,

then taped it to the bottom of his car." Mila glowed with pride as she put the car in park and turned to face them.

"Damn. That was Penny levels of clever." Penny nodded in agreement with two thumbs up.

Mila frowned, looking at Finn's face.

"Hang on. I'll be right back." She got out of the car and walked into the convenience store.

Finn watched her go, noticing for the first time that she wasn't wearing her jacket and had the corset on full display. He had to admit that it fit her well.

He glanced into the back seat while Penny played with the settings on the tracking app. He reached back and pulled Mila's torn jacket to the front seat.

"Shir?" Penny asked, touching the jacket where it was torn down the side.

"Yeah, I think she left a little something out of that story." He tossed the ruined jacket into the back and squinted down at the screen. "Where's he going?"

Penny shrugged, zooming out to reveal most of the city as if to say "Anywhere."

The door opened, and Mila climbed back into the driver's seat, holding a white plastic bag. She pulled out a wad of napkins and a bottle of water. She cracked the bottle open with a twist of the plastic cap and proceeded to soak a couple of napkins before leaning over and gently pulling Finn's hand away from his face.

"Let me help you." She shook her head, her expression serious as she began blotting the blood in his beard and on his cheeks. "You're a mess."

At least the bleeding from his nose had stopped, but he could still taste copper in the back of his throat.

She was gentle around his nose and eye but got in deep when it came to his beard, trying to get the blood out before it dried. She had to change out the napkins several times before they started coming away relatively clean.

She gave him an odd look. "Have you not taken a healing potion?"

Finn shook his head. "I don't have any left. Penny took one to give to you at the garage, and the other was broken in the fight."

"How did it break if it was in your holster?"

"Well, my holster is just leather. I mean, it's tough leather, but when a tire iron slams into it with an orc's strength behind it, it just can't hold up. The vial shattered in its pocket." He leaned back so she could get a better angle.

"Here," she reached around and pulled her potion out to hand it to him. "Take mine. I'm pretty sure your nose is broken."

He pushed it away. "No. You hang onto it. I'll be fine. I can take one later when we get home. I don't want us to end up needing the potion, and not having it because of this. I'm not in any danger of dying. It's just going to suck for a little bit. Put it away. That's our last one, and it's only lunchtime."

She obviously didn't like the solution, but she nodded and slipped the potion back into the pocket of her corset. "Okay, but you take one as soon as we get home."

He smiled. "Yes, Mom."

She rolled her eyes and checked him over one more time. "Okay, you still look like an undercooked ham, but at least you're not covered in blood anymore. How's our tracker doing, Penny?"

"Chi chi." Penny held up the phone, and they could see that the other car was now on 25 South and was making pretty good time.

"Okay, let's go. Maybe we can finally figure out who the fuck has these hounds." Mila started the car and pulled back onto the main road, heading for 85 South.

Within minutes, they were cruising down the freeway, the car they were following leading by a good ten or fifteen minutes. That gap was closing, thanks to Mila's lead foot.

"Hey, I want to give Anita a call," Finn said, thinking about the orcs that had been attacked.

"Sure. The phone is already connected to the car's Bluetooth. Penny, open the recent calls, and she should be at the top."

After a couple of seconds, they could hear the sound of the phone connecting through the speakers.

"Hello? Who is this?" Anita's tight voice answered.

"Anita, it's Finn."

"Oh." Her voice lost its tightness and went straight to put-out. "What do you want?"

Finn frowned, and he and Mila made eye contact, both raising an eyebrow at her tone.

"Well, I had a question about the hellhounds, but if you're busy…"

Anita cut him off. "I am busy, thanks to you. You fed my poor hound too much fucking meat, and she's sick. If I can keep you from doing something like that again, then ask your question. Otherwise, I don't really have the time."

"Well," Finn cleared his throat, feeling guilty about the

meat. "I need to know if a hound can imprint on more than one person. And how it works. Do they follow your orders no matter what, or are there limitations to what you can get them to do?"

Anita sighed as if he were some sort of child. "Of course, a hound can't imprint twice, that's the whole point of imprinting; it's for life. And no, a hound won't do *anything* you tell it to. For example, it won't jump off a cliff; it has a sense of self-preservation, after all."

"How long does it take a hound to imprint?" he asked, trying to make the timing work in his head even before he heard the answer.

"They have to imprint right after birth. Maybe up to a week after, but any more than that, and the chances of it being permanent goes down quickly. I would say nine to ten days at most." They could hear her fiddling with a set of keys in the background, then the sound of barking hounds nearly blew out the speakers. "Hang on, I'm going into my office."

The barking was suddenly cut off.

"Is that all you needed?"

Finn frowned. Her attitude was not making him any less suspicious, but then again, she was upset at him about her sick hound, so he let it slide a little. "Actually, I have one more question. Let's say you have some hounds you need to control, but they're not imprinted to you. How would you control them?"

"Meat," she said simply before taking a bite of something and chewing loudly.

"I'm talking about a little more than moving them from one cage to another." Finn was getting sick and tired of her attitude. "How would you control them like they were bound to you? Could you use mind control through magic or an artifact of some kind?"

The line was filled with crunching. It went on so long that Finn thought she wasn't going to answer the question.

He'd opened his mouth to ask if she was still there when she answered, "I suppose you could use some sort of mind control, but if you're talking about controlling the whole litter, it would have to be one hell of a spell." She took another bite but continued around the mouthful in a muffled voice. "I would say you could use an artifact, but again it would have to be something really powerful. Probably dwarven-made and powered by someone who knew what the hell they were doing. One slip and the hounds would turn on the user in an instant. Well, actually, it might stun them at first, but the hounds are smart. They would know they had been controlled and try to put a stop to it."

"So, if it's an artifact, and we can stop the user, what does that mean for the hounds? Will they have to be put down?" Finn didn't like that idea. It wasn't like they had chosen any of this.

Anita crunched through another bite before answering. "They would be a handful for a while, but eventually they would calm back down. Taking care of them will be a bitch, though. They'll basically be wild animals at that point, but *I* could do it." She seemed to be saying the last thought to herself more than to them.

"Thanks, Anita. That should be helpful. I'll try not to kill the hounds, but no promises." Finn hung up before he could hear her reply.

"I still can't tell if she's a part of this or not." Mila shook her head in disbelief. "I hope she's just got horrendous people skills and isn't an accessory to murder. She seems to really like animals, maybe a little more than the people around them."

"Yeah, I've known a few people like that," Finn agreed, pulling up the tracking app again. "I'm hoping she's innocent just because we don't have another hellhound expert on hand, but I'm not holding my breath." He zoomed in on the map and squinted, his swollen eye making it hard to read the tiny road names. "Looks like he's getting off the freeway. He's turning north on South Colorado Boulevard."

Mila put her turn signal on, making her way to the exit lane. "That's the next exit. Looks like we caught up with him."

"Don't get too close," Finn warned. "We don't want him to spot us."

"He's still a few minutes ahead of us," she said, pulling onto the exit ramp and slowing down for the light. "Don't worry, I don't want to get you into a fight any more than you want one." She gave him a sad smile, looking at his face.

A few minutes later, the car turned off the main road and onto East Exposition Avenue. Mila was getting more and more agitated the further they went.

"Are you okay?" Finn raised an eyebrow at her obvious discomfort.

"I just have a pretty good idea where he's going."

"Really? Where?" he asked, squinting down at the map in Penny's hands.

"Polo Club," was all she said.

Finn had no idea what a Polo Club was until he noticed it was the name of the street the car pulled onto. He didn't see what the big deal was until he noticed that the outlines of the house lots on the map were way too big. Like, ten times too big for a normal house. These were estates, not houses.

"Yeah, he's turning down Polo Club Circle right now. I mean, they're big houses, but what's the big deal?"

She sighed. "Well, it's a private neighborhood. They have their own security patrolling the roads. Not exactly a lot of street parking. If we stop, they'll come and investigate."

"Okay, then we don't stop for too long." He smiled. "And don't go racing through the streets like you normally do."

She gave him a dark look. "What's the point of a fast car if you can't drive fast?"

"The knowledge that you can if you want."

CHAPTER TWENTY

Mila kept the car basically at idle, not making too much noise, and cruising along at about fifteen miles an hour. They started to pass a tall, white fence on their left, and it took them a second to realize it was the fence to the house they were looking for. Coming to the driveway, they could see that the fence encircled the entire property and had a large iron gate that looked as impressive as the one at Preston's.

The small glimpse they caught on the drive by the house was impressive. It was three stories and topped with steep, angled, slate roofing. There were several black cars in the drive, but the tan sedan they had been following was parked among them. Then all they could see was more white wall.

Despite what Mila had said about there not being street parking, there were several more black cars parked along the street in front of the house. Mostly mean-looking sedans, but a few Suburbans were thrown into the mix as if there was a government party happening at the house, and no one knew how to carpool.

"Well, that would be the most impressive thing I've seen today if I hadn't already watched Penny set a warehouse on fire." Mila chuckled, putting a little more gas to the engine, and taking the road back out toward the entrance to the neighborhood.

"Head back around and park behind the cars on the street. We need a little more info on what we're dealing with." Finn frowned at the phone screen in Penny's hands. "Penny, is there a way to get a view of this place that's more than just a map? Like a top view of what's actually there?"

She shrugged and started fiddling with the settings until she found a toggle to turn on the satellite view, then began scrolling across the city to find where they were. Mila made the turn to stay on the circle and idled back down the street toward the white-walled estate. She slipped the Hellcat into the first vacant spot behind a sedan and shut the car off.

"Can't see much." She sat up in her seat as far as she could and squinted.

They had a view of the gate, but basically, all they could see beyond that was the large turnaround in front of the house.

After a few seconds, a pair of guards walked across the drive on their side of the gate, a man and a woman, both in black tactical gear and chatting with one another. Finn didn't see any obvious weapons, so he figured they must be magic users, which meant they were more than likely Kashgar, not Peabrains.

Penny held up the phone. "Chi." A small puff of smoke filtered out from between her teeth in frustration.

Finn and Mila leaned in, but the image was just a gray blob with the word UNAVAILABLE written across it.

Mila raised an eyebrow. "Well, that's not something you see very often. Most military installations have a filter on them, but I've never seen a private residence filtered out. Someone paid a lot of money to make that happen."

"Can we find out who the house belongs to?" he asked.

Mila gave that a moment's thought. "Maybe." She took the phone and opened a browser, typing into the search bar. "It's a private residence, but it should be in the public tax records. Give me a second."

Finn watched the front gate for signs they'd been detected, but it seemed that the black Hellcat was similar enough to the other sedans that they were going unnoticed by the chatting guards.

On a whim, he rolled down the window and listened.

Mila shivered at the cold air flowing in. "Dude, it's freezing. Roll that up."

Finn pulled off his bomber jacket, sucking in a breath against the sudden pain in his ribs, but he hid the accompanying grimace by turning away. He didn't want Mila to worry too much.

She reached over and helped him get the jacket off.

"Thanks. Here, put this on." He handed her the jacket and leaned out the window a little to listen.

She shrugged into the way-too-big jacket and rolled up the sleeves a few turns to keep her hands free. "What are you listening for?"

"Well, every time we were in the hound sanctuary at the

Menagerie, the hounds were barking and howling. I assume the ones we're looking for would do the same thing."

"Yeah, but I thought they were being controlled by a spell or something. Wouldn't whoever's in charge keep them quiet?"

Finn glanced at Mila and suppressed a smile. She was absolutely adorable in his oversized (for her) coat. "The spell would have to be extremely powerful, so I imagine it would only last for a short period. That's one of the reasons I think they're using an artifact, and probably a dwarven-made one, if it's powerful enough to hold more than twenty hellhounds in its thrall. Something that powerful would be extra taxing for a non-dwarf to harness because they can't channel the raw magic trapped in the ground that's needed to power it properly. So, the same problem applies. They would only be able to use it for short periods of time; maybe an hour at most before it burnt them out."

"Shir shi!" Penny held up a hand to quiet them down as she stood on Finn's leg and leaned out the open window, her eyes closed.

"She hears dogs barking," Finn whispered, keeping Mila in the loop.

They waited while she listened, Finn closing his eyes as well to try and heighten his hearing. After a few minutes, he could make out the distant barking, but if the wind shifted even slightly, he lost it.

Mila continued to look up information on the house while Penny's face became frustrated.

Finally, the faerie dragon pulled herself back into the

car and huffed. "Squee. Shirch serie?" She put her hands on her hips and raised a questioning eye ridge.

Finn shook his head. "I don't want you flying in there alone. We have no idea how many wards they have in place. They could spot you and take you out, and we would never know."

She nodded but countered with "Grich, shi."

Finn pursed his lips, then nodded. "Fine, but get some height before you approach. And if we have to get out of here, keep an eye on the car and meet us once we're out of the neighborhood."

She gave him a firm nod, then crawled out of the window and launched herself with a kick off the door. She glided low to the ground until she disappeared into the bushes across the street.

"What's she doing?" Mila asked, clicking on a link on her phone.

"She's going to take a look at the place from a couple of hundred feet up. We figure if they have any wards, they won't extend that high, because of plane travel." He bit his thumbnail, then leaned over and pulled open the jacket Mila was wearing, reaching into the opening.

"Hey! What the hell?" She yelped before realizing he was pulling his box of Charleston Chews from the inside pocket. "You could warn a girl before diving into her jacket."

"Technically, it's my jacket," he gave her a half-smile and then opened the box. "I'm just a little nervous for her. I hate it when she goes out on her own like this."

"She's an independent woman. She can handle herself better than both of us." Mila squinted down at what she had found. "Besides, doesn't she do stuff like this all the time?"

"This is different." He sighed, craning his neck to try and pick her out against the bright blue sky. "Normally, I could get to her if something happens, but this is a little more out there. We can't just go charging in. They could have an army in there. If the number of vehicles is any indication, then that statement isn't an exaggeration."

"Found it!" Mila held the phone out, but the text was so small, he couldn't read it with his eye swollen like it was. She realized he was having trouble and read it for him. "It says that three months ago, the property was privately owned by some guy and his wife, but then it was sold to a corporation called Black Hole Consulting."

Finn raised an eyebrow. "Black Hole Consulting? Could they be any more obvious? It's the Dark Star." He glanced toward the gate, and his eyes widened. "Oh shit. The guards are coming this way."

The two guards were walking beside the wall, and the woman was looking directly at the car. She pointed at them. "Hold it right there! What are you doing out here?"

She approached the car cautiously, while the guy with her took up a defensive stance and took a few quick steps to the side to spread them out.

Now that they were close, Finn could tell they were both Kashgar, and the way they held their hands at the ready told him they were both capable casters.

"Shit. Get us out of here. The last thing we want is a fight in the street when they have backup just around the corner," Finn said, preparing his own spell in the back of his mind.

Mila rolled down her window and held up her phone. "Hey, we're lost. I was just looking up directions."

The two guards relaxed visibly, and the woman stepped closer, bending down and resting her arms on the opening as she leaned in closer to Mila.

"Well, pretty little lady, this is a private neighborhood. You can't be here, though I might make an exception for you." She gave Mila a coy smile before glancing up and seeing Finn for the first time, his face purple and bruised, with one eye half swollen shut. "Jesus! What the fuck happened to you?" She leaned in further, narrowing her eyes. "Wait, you're that fucking dwarf!"

Her hand came up, glittering golden light forming around her palm, along with a small, translucent bubble.

Mila jammed her elbow up into the woman's nose, eliciting a crunch and a splash of blood that hit the ceiling of the car. The woman screamed, falling back and clutching her face. Her partner didn't even bother to check on her, just stepped closer to the Hellcat, a determined look on his face, and a bubble of magic on his fingertips.

Finn reached across Mila and pointed his palm at the man as it began to glow with purple light.

"*Gunna salainn!*" he shouted, and a tight grouping of salt crystals blasted out like from a shotgun, tearing into the man's hand and fingers before shredding his black jacket and knocking him backward, his magic fizzling out as he flew.

Mila started the car and hit the gas, peeling out onto the road, and fishtailing for a second before taking the long curve and moving out of view of the estate. She had to swerve to avoid hitting a Mercedes SUV turning into the neighborhood, causing her to slide out onto the main road and almost get sideswiped by a car before she straightened out again.

Finn looked over his shoulder but didn't see any cars following them. He then scanned the sky, looking for Penny, but she was either too far away or flying at some angle that made her difficult to see.

Mila slowed at the stoplight on Colorado Boulevard, checking her mirrors, and breathing hard.

Penny swooped in through Finn's open window, making him jump and Mila flinch.

She landed on his lap, breathing hard, but held up a thumb and smiled. "Chi chi." She then took the box of Chews from Finn's hand and tipped it into her open mouth.

Finn let her have the rest of the box, knowing that using as much power as she had to catch up would make her hungrier than usual. If there was one thing he had learned over the years, it was not to get between a hungry dragon and its meal.

"You okay?" Finn asked Mila, who was still a little wide-eyed.

"Yeah. I'm good." She barked a laugh. "This shit is exciting! I love it."

Finn had to laugh at her exuberance. He was glad she was having a good time, but things were about to get serious. "Okay, but now we have a problem. They now know we know where they are. So that means they're probably going to move the hounds or get reinforcements, or both. We need to move soon. I'm thinking tonight we try and get in there."

"What's the plan? Kill the hounds, or take out the leader? Either way, we still have all the guards to deal with," Mila argued, making the turn onto Colorado Boulevard to head north.

"We'll have to come up with something. But first things first, we need to talk to Preston and give him the ring. Maybe he'll have some ideas."

"No." Mila made a chopping motion. "The first thing we'll do is stop by the house and get a few healing potions. No need to go in half-cocked if we don't have to. Besides, the condo is on our way to Preston's...sort of."

Finn wanted to tell her that time was against them at this point, but he had to agree that he was not exactly in fighting shape with his broken ribs.

He nodded. "Good idea. We should be prepared for anything."

They rode in silence for a few minutes before Mila started chuckling.

"What?"

"I'm pretty sure that guard was trying to hit on me until she saw you."

Finn raised an eyebrow. "She works for an evil overlord."

Mila shrugged. "It's just nice to know I've still got it."

CHAPTER TWENTY-ONE

Finn relaxed on the couch, holding the now empty healing potion bottle, and winced ever so slightly as his ribs knit back together. Mila was right; he'd needed the potion. He was in so much pain that he hadn't realized just how bad it had been. He wouldn't be surprised if he'd had some internal bleeding from the tire iron to his side.

Mila knelt on the couch next to him, watching his face with rapt attention. She jumped, her hand going to her mouth, as Finn's nose cracked loudly, resetting itself.

His nose resetting was a bit much and made his eyes tear up.

Penny, who had seen this show a hundred times, was holding a notebook, trying to draw what she had seen on her brief scouting mission. She was even putting down where she saw guards and what she thought their patrol probably looked like from the short time she saw them moving.

"How do you feel?" Mila winced as the broken skin around his eye sealed itself back up.

"Better." He sat up, turning his head to the side and getting a satisfying crack from his stiff neck. "The healing potion stop was a good call. Speaking of calls, can you reach out to Preston to see when he's available?"

Mila sat back on the couch, her feet tucked under her, and pulled out her phone. "Sure. Do you have his card?"

Finn reached into his back pocket and pulled out both Preston's and Anita's cards. He handed Preston's to Mila and was about to put Anita's away when her number caught his eye. He wasn't a genius when it came to numbers, but the first three-digit sequence looked familiar to him and he frowned at the card, trying to think of where he had seen it before.

His eyes widened. "No. It can't be that easy. Where's Peter's phone?"

Mila lifted her hips and pulled the smartphone from her back pocket, unlocking it before handing it to him. "What is it?" She had Preston's number punched in but hadn't called yet.

"I think I recognize this number." He shook Anita's card with one hand as he used the other to access the texts on Peter's phone.

"I mean, we've called her twice today," Mila said, biting her lip, her thumb hovering over the call button.

"*I* never saw the number," he pointed out. "You called her first, then we just hit redial when we called from the car." She stared at her phone in hesitation. "Just call. He's just another person, and we're working for him. He gave us the card so we *could* call him."

"Yeah, well, excuse me for feeling nervous about calling one of the most powerful men in the world."

"I'm really glad my pedigree doesn't mean anything here on *Earth*. I might never have met you because you would have been too nervous to talk to me." He reached over and hit the call button for her.

She looked up at him, her eyes wide with betrayal. "I can't believe you did that!"

He laughed. "You better get on that call. Wouldn't want him to have to wait."

She gasped and put the phone to her ear.

Finn smiled at her then went back to the contacts in Peter's phone. He checked the D, J, and A without any luck, but when he opened the K, his heart jumped a little. He compared the numbers, and they were the same. K was Anita, or at least, K had been using her number.

Just to be sure, he checked the date of the last text from K on the phone and saw that it was the day before the theft, a little over two months ago.

"Hello?" Mila's voice was shaky as she spoke into the phone, but she straightened up after a second. "Oh, hello, this is Dr. Winters." She had a slightly disappointed look on her face and gave Finn an embarrassed shrug. "Finn and I have found the ring. When would be a good time to come see Mr. Meriwether?" She waited a second for the reply before continuing. "Well, tonight would be better. We have a lead we would like to talk to him about, but it's time-sensitive."

She pulled the phone away from her ear and covered the microphone with her other hand. "It's the butler. He's checking with Preston."

"And you thought he was going to answer the phone himself." Finn laughed. "I've been around many rich and powerful people, and the only thing they had in common besides their wealth was the fact that they didn't do even the simplest things for themselves, like answering the phone."

"He said it was his personal number," she argued.

"It is. It literally is the number for his house. That alone is pretty impressive."

The muffled sound of talking made Mila quickly press the phone back to her ear. "Yeah, I'm here...okay, great. We'll be there soon." She hung up and smiled. "He said to come over now."

She grabbed her boots from beside the couch and zipped them on before getting up. She then went to the closet and grabbed her short, dark-red leather coat. Finn liked it better than the black one, especially with the black corset underneath, and might have secretly been glad that her black one had been ripped to shreds.

He got up and unrolled the sleeves of his haggard bomber jacket before slipping it on. When he was done, Mila was already propping the front door open, waiting for him.

"Come on, let's go-o-o-o." She impatiently waved for him to hurry.

"Hold your horses, little doggy."

He glared at her playfully as he made a detour to the refrigerator and opened the freezer, pulling out a fresh box of Charleston Chews Minis. He shook the box at her as he passed by, through the door.

"Now I'm ready. Where's Penny?"

Penny gave a toot, ripped the sheet of paper she had been making the map on from the notebook, took off from the table, and soared through the open door, landing on Finn's shoulder.

"Are we all ready *now*?" Mila glared at them.

Finn just laughed. "Money does weird things to you Peabrains."

"I just don't want Preston to have to sit around waiting for us. He's a very busy man." She locked the door and led the way to the elevator.

"Trust me, Preston isn't sitting around waiting on us."

"Chire shir." Penny laughed.

Finn chuckled. "She bet you five bucks that we'll have to wait at least half an hour to see him."

Mila frowned at the little blue dragon. "You're on. But if I win, you have to give me a head massage. Those talons of yours are like magic on my scalp. And none of that five-minute shit. I want a full half-hour."

Penny smiled and held out her small hand, which Mila reached up and shook.

"Well, I got out of that pretty easy." Finn beamed at her.

She elbowed him. "Not even. You'll be working on my feet with those big thumbs of yours."

They rode the elevator down, and after a couple of seconds, Mila turned to Finn, her head cocked to the side. "Did you call me 'little doggy?'"

Kal stepped to the side after opening the large oak door, gesturing for them to enter.

"Please come in. Mister Meriwether is waiting for you in his office."

Mila elbowed Finn again, this time eliciting an *oof* from him. "See? I told you."

He chuckled and nodded. "You win this one, Doctor Winters."

She rolled her eyes and stepped in, followed by Finn and Penny. Kal led them through the house, his hooves on the wooden floors muffled by some sort of rubberized horseshoe. Eventually, he led them to a set of double doors, opened them both, and stepped to the side to let the trio pass.

"Mister Meriwether, your guests have arrived," he announced.

"Thank you, Kal."

Preston was sitting at a huge, wooden desk situated in front of a set of large, arching windows, dark now that the sun had set, but reflecting firelight from the roaring fireplace at the side of the living- room-sized office. He had been playing on his phone but put the device down when his guests entered, and Finn was surprised to see the same game that Mila liked to play.

"Thanks for seeing us on such short notice," Mila said, her confidence soaring with her victory.

"No, thank you for resolving the issue so quickly." He gestured to the large, plush leather chairs facing his desk. "Please, have a seat. Would you like a drink?" he asked, walking over to the wet bar and making himself a whiskey on the rocks.

"I'll have one of those if you don't mind," Finn said, never one to decline a free drink.

"And for you two?" Preston turned to Mila and Penny,

the tongs in his hand holding a large, round ice ball above a rocks glass.

"I'll have the same." Mila shrugged.

Finn could tell that she would prefer her G&T but didn't want to put Preston out.

Not one to worry about such things herself, Penny took off and landed beside Preston on the wet bar and began to peruse his selection, one hand on her hip, and the other tapping at her chin. Preston smiled down at her, obviously enjoying her authenticity. She eventually found something she liked, a fifty-year-old scotch, and tapped the bottle, then pointed at the ice and shook her head.

Preston gave her a half-bow. "You have good taste, my lady. It's the most expensive thing on the shelf."

He chuckled at her nonchalant shrug, then poured their drinks as Penny swooped back over to the table. She realized a small bowl of mints sat in the center, and tossed a few in her mouth, crunching them up just in time for Preston to put her very expensive drink down beside her. He handed both Mila and Finn their drinks and went back to his chair, taking a sip of his own drink before setting the glass down.

"Okay, now that we're all comfortable." He leaned forward, folding his massive hands on the desk in front of him. "What have you learned?"

Finn pulled out Peter's phone, having Mila unlock it before he slid it to Preston across the big desk. "This is the phone of the guy who stole the hound. There are only four numbers saved on it, each identified only by a single letter, but if you look under the contact info for 'K,' you'll find

Anita's number. The last message was received just before the break-in, but it's looking like she's the inside man."

Preston scrolled quickly through the phone, much more familiar with the tech than Finn was. He sighed when he got to Anita's number. "While this does look damning, I can't believe she would put her animals in danger. She's a little hard to get along with, but all she cares about are her charges, particularly the hounds."

He sat back, considering for a few minutes.

"This is her work number."

Finn took a sip of his whiskey and raised his eyebrows in appreciation at its superior taste. "Is that important?"

"Well, we just switched phones for all the employees a few months ago. I remember Anita was complaining that she didn't get hers right away. I thought it had been a missed order, but now I'm thinking someone was holding her phone and using it to frame her. She's too smart to use one of *my* phones to betray me. It's just a little too obvious." He reached up and absentmindedly scratched at the base of one of his large horns. "I'll be sure to keep an eye on her, but I think this is a red herring."

"Well, we thought we should bring it up, just in case," Mila said, setting her untouched drink on the table. "Did you hear about the Selkies and Orcs who were attacked?"

Preston nodded. "I did. I assume you talked to them?"

"Yeah, the Selkies were as helpful as they could be, but the Orcs decided to start a fight with Finn before he got too much from them."

Finn picked up the story for her. "I did get one piece of info that's pretty important. It looks like the Dark Star or her agents now have the hounds, and they have a way to control them, at least to a degree. Thanks to Mila's quick thinking, we tracked one of her agents from the orcs' shop to an estate on Polo Club Circle. Huge place with white stone walls surrounding it."

Preston's head cocked to the side. "The Gerivaldie Estate? I know it. But that makes no sense, Fred and his wife are just Peabrains. They don't have a connection to the Dark Star in any way."

"I looked up the public record." Mila pulled out her phone and brought up the web page before handing it to Preston. "It says it was sold to Black Hole Consulting not long ago."

Preston read the document, his face becoming dark with anger. "I swear to God, if that fucking bitch hurt those two, I'll hunt her to the ends of the Earth. The Gerivaldies were one of the most philanthropic families in the country. They gave away billions over the years to help people all over the world. They would never hurt a fly."

"We have a little more," Finn said, scooting forward in his chair. "We know the hounds are at the estate now, but we were spotted while scoping the place out, and I think they're going to move them. We want to try and get in tonight, but we're a little lost as to what we should do once we're there. Obviously, we can't let the hounds be used as a weapon against the public, but I don't really want to go in there and try to kill a pack of stone-skinned hounds. I'm pretty sure whoever has them is using some sort of mind control artifact. If we can get our hands on that, then we might be able to end this before it really starts."

Preston took another sip of whiskey before answering, weighing his words. "If it were me, I would just go for the leader, but we don't really know who that is. What we need is information. I have a small strike team I can call on, but they're currently on another mission, and at least a few hours out. We could take the estate by force, but I'm not going to send my people in blind. Would you be able to get in and do a little scouting? It would be helpful to know for sure if an artifact is controlling them. Gives us a target to go after."

"We can get in," Finn shrugged. "But if there's an opportunity for us to get the artifact ourselves, I'm going to take it."

"I agree, but do be careful. I don't want—"

The glass of both windows behind Preston exploded inward, shards flying into the room. One speared the table, only inches from Penny, who jumped to the side with a squeak.

Preston jumped to his feet, his eyes dark with anger and his shoulders flexing. "What the fucking hell?"

Four men dressed in hoods and tactical gear jumped through the busted windows, chains of small bubbles flying from the hands of two of them and wrapping around Preston, pinning his arms and legs.

Finn grabbed the coffee table between him and Mila and threw it at one of the attackers, sending Penny into the air and circling in for an attack. The table exploded, its target holding his hand up shooting a bolt of light.

"Don't suppose you guys want to talk it out?" Finn asked, reaching back and grabbing the handle of Fragar.

The four intruders leaped at him and Mila.

"Good."

Finn let the rage loose and sprinted to meet them.

CHAPTER TWENTY-TWO

Finn punched an assassin in the face, his rage-fueled state making him stronger than he had any right to be and sending the hooded attacker rag-dolling end over end, his neck at an unnatural angle.

The rage flowed through him, only held back by his worry for Mila and his need to protect her. He glanced to the side to see that she had pulled Gram out and was chopping at her attacker, her second attacker, not noticing the sword and thinking her less of a threat, tried to flank Finn.

Finn gave a whispered word, and Fragar unfolded, glowing blue runes flashing with power. He threw the axe overhand at the flanker, taking him square in the chest. The assassin screamed and collapsed to the ground, leaving behind a smear of blood as his momentum slid him across the polished wooden floor.

Finn turned back just in time to see the second of his initial attackers swinging down a metal rod, crackling with energy. Finn threw up an arm in defense and took the magical weapon's blow. The impact sent sparks flying and instantly numbed his arm. It fell to his side, useless for the moment.

Instead of retreating, Finn stepped into the attack, leaned forward, and drove his forehead into the assassin's face. He heard a satisfying crunch of cartilage as the hooded man stumbled back.

Penny swooped past him, breathing a thin line of fire as she went, presumably to help Mila with the last man. Finn felt almost cheated that the attack was over so soon.

The hooded man in front of him put a hand to his face mask, blood dripping through the black fabric as he cautiously took a step back.

"Got ya now, little man," Finn growled, advancing another step.

The assassin looked over his shoulder at the broken windows.

"Thinkin' a' runnin'?" Finn's berserker rage didn't make him eloquent.

The assassin lowered his hand to the metal rod, holding it like a two-handed sword. "Not exactly, dwarf."

Four more assassins came flying in through the window, already charging magical attacks aimed at Finn and Mila.

Finn opened his mouth to roar but was beaten to it by Preston. The Minotaur's roar shook the room, vibrating the bottles on the wet bar, drawing the attention of everyone in the room. Finn took the opportunity to throw the leather chair he had been sitting in at the man he faced.

The last of the original attackers never saw the furniture missile coming, and was thrown back into one of the newcomers, whose spell exploded into his partner, killing him instantly. The caster then stumbled back from the force of the impact and was impaled through the back by a piece of glass still clinging to the window frame.

The second newcomer had sidestepped the incoming chair and unfurled a string of tiny bubbles that formed a burning whip, coiled at his feet. With a graceful arcing motion, the whip slipped into the air before snapping forward at incredible speed, slashing at the still restrained Minotaur and leaving a burning line across his chest.

Finn glanced over and saw Preston flexing huge shoulder muscles, putting enormous strain on his magical bindings. He roared again, his eyes erupting in flame as he released his magic, and the bubbles binding him were ripped apart. Froth dripped from his mouth, and smoke snorted from his flaring nostrils.

The burning whip slashed again, this time across Preston's face, making him turn away, but he snapped his head back around to pierce his target with his hellish gaze. Finn almost felt bad for the assassin as Preston tossed his huge wooden desk to the side with one arm, and charged the now-backpedaling assassin, head lowered and horns bursting into flames.

Finn wanted to see what happened next but was distracted by the sight of Mila on her butt, Gram held defensively in front of her as a thin tendril of smoke rose from her chest. Finn saw that her original assailant was down, staring with dead eyes, his face half-charred by dragon fire and blood pooling under him from a slash across his chest.

The two remaining men quickly took stock of the situation and rightly determined they had no chance of winning the fight. As if on some unheard cue, they both turned and ran for the window.

Finn sprang the short distance to where Fragar protruded from the chest of one of the dead men and snatched the handle up, spun, and threw it again. His aim was slightly off, due to his numb arm affecting his balance, but he was able to take the arm off the assassin closest to the window. The man spun and screamed in pain. His partner ran into his back, and they both went down in a heap.

Finn took a deep breath, quelling his rage, knowing in the back of his mind that they needed to question these men. He was taking his second deep breath when the sound of pounding hooves made him spin and put up his good arm in a defensive posture.

Preston was charging straight at him. He acted quickly, rolling out of his way and coming up on one knee just in time to see the Minotaur slam into both remaining assassins, crushing them into the bookshelf. The sound of cracking bones and the spray of blood across the book spines was all the evidence Finn needed to know that they were dead.

Penny landed on Finn's shoulder, pulling back a large portion of his rage with a cool hand to his cheek, but Finn was focused on Preston. Minotaurs were similar to berserkers in that they tended to get carried away in battle, and Finn had no desire to face down an enraged one.

Preston stood over the mangled bodies, his shoulders heaving, and horns still flaming. Slowly, the flames died down until they finally flickered out, but Preston still didn't turn Finn's direction; he just stood over the bodies, breathing heavily.

Finn was impressed that Preston was able to pull himself back from the edge. It spoke volumes about how powerful he actually was. Most Minotaurs would be stuck in their rage for days, destroying everything they came across. Their fear of killing innocents while in this state was the main reason they didn't mingle with other races.

Mila stepped up to Finn's side, her hand slipping into his. "Are you okay?"

Finn nodded and glanced down at her. Besides a small burnt spot on her t-shirt, she looked fine. "You?"

"Yeah." She watched Preston's internal battle rage on. "Is he?"

Finn considered for a few more seconds before nodding. "I think so. But let's not interrupt, just in case."

After another ten seconds, Preston stood up to his full height and straightened his suit jacket. He turned to face them, and Finn was glad to see that his eyes had returned to their normal coloring.

"Sorry about that." He cleared his throat and pulled a white handkerchief from his inside pocket and dabbed at his forehead, the cloth coming away red. His brown fur had hidden the fact that he was covered in blood. "It seemed you needed the help." He held up the handkerchief and chuckled. "This is the problem with my head being my main weapon. It's messy."

The doors burst open, and Finn and Mila spun, Finn raising his fists, and Mila readying Gram. They relaxed a bit when they saw it was only Kal. However, Finn did a double-take when he saw that the centaur held an automatic rifle in his hands.

Several men came in behind him in black suits, each of them wearing earpieces, having the look of private security.

"It's fine, Kal," Preston said in a calm, authoritative manner. "Our friends here took good care of me. Though, I have to ask, how is it that these assassins made it this far onto the property without setting off any of the wards?"

"We're not sure, sir." Kal lowered his rifle and gave a slight bow. "I'm having our people look into it as we speak."

"Fine, do your sweeps, and get our people to clean this up. I'll show our guests out."

Kal gave another half-bow and ushered the security detail out of the room, backing out behind them.

Preston held out a hand toward the open door. "I'm sorry you had to be a part of that. It's rare that I'm attacked anymore, but it does happen, unfortunately. You should probably go before this place turns into a zoo of cleaners and guards, combing every inch of the property."

They headed out into the hall, and Finn cleared his throat. "Actually, those guys were probably after us. We were attacked by someone very similar earlier today."

Preston raised an eyebrow. "Why didn't you mention that before?"

Finn shrugged. "I wasn't sure it had anything to do with the hunt for the hounds. I figured it was just the Dark Star coming after us because we keep asking questions. Though, now that we know she's connected to the hound's theft, I guess I should have mentioned it. It kind of slipped my mind."

"How often do you get attacked that you forget about assassins attacking you?" Preston asked, his eyes wide.

Finn shrugged again. "More often than you would think, probably. Although, I do have to say the number has gone down considerably since I arrived here on *Earth*."

They walked to the main foyer, and Preston stopped them at the door. "You two be careful." He turned to Finn. "You're good in a fight, and I think you're a good man who I would like to keep working with. You did the job I asked and did it quickly and with minimal collateral damage."

"That was mostly by accident," Finn admitted. "Just a fair warning, for future jobs, collateral damage is kind of my specialty."

Preston chuckled. "I'll keep that in mind." His face became serious again. "I'm going to start putting more resources into looking into the Dark Star and what she has planned. She was in my periphery, but I had no idea her movement had gained so much traction so quickly. I also need to investigate my employees. It's obvious to me now that I have a traitor in my house. I'll start with Anita, but I really think that's a false lead."

"Do what you have to. So, can we count on backup at the Gerivaldie estate if we find what we're looking for?"

Preston nodded. "Yes, but as I said, it will be a few hours before they can get here, so be careful until then."

"Finn!"

They turned to see Anita jogging from the back of the house with a scoped rifle in her hands.

Finn pulled Fragar out and pushed Mila behind him.

Anita slid to a stop, a shocked look on her face as the axe unfolded. "What the fuck?" she yelled, holding the rifle across her chest as if trying to hide behind it.

"You have a rifle! What do you mean 'what the fuck'?" he shouted, confused.

Preston stepped between them and held a hand up to Finn. "Sorry, I completely forgot in the midst of the attack. I asked Anita to bring you something you can use to take the hounds out safely."

Anita quickly handed Preston the gun and a shoulder bag that clanked when its contents shifted, then stepped back still eyeing Fragar.

Finn, feeling slightly embarrassed but completely justified, put Fragar away. "Sorry, it's been a stressful few hours."

"Apparently," Anita said, shaking slightly with fright at almost being chopped down. "Anyway, this is the best I could come up with on short notice. It's a tranq gun that uses a magical firing mechanism, so it's pretty quiet. We have a few tranquilizer darts that might have enough punch to get through the stone skin, maybe thirty or forty in all. They're in the bag."

"'Might have enough punch'?" Finn raised an eyebrow.

She shrugged. "Never tried them on stone skin specifically, but they'll go through a basilisk's skin, and those things are pretty tough."

"Okay." Finn took the gun and bag from Preston. "Thanks."

"Whatever." She turned and stomped out the back, her hands still shaking slightly as she pulled out a cigarette and her lighter before rounding a corner and moving out of sight.

"I really don't think it's her. I've known her for far too long, and I have never seen her do anything that would put one of her animals in danger," Preston said again, turning back to the door and pulling it open for them.

"Yeah, maybe," Finn relented. "Well, we'll call in when we find anything."

"Good luck." He shook Finn's hand, then gave Penny a small bow before finally taking Mila's hand. "Do be careful, Dr. Winters. These are not friendly people."

"I will. Thanks, Preston." She smiled up at him, then stepped out the door.

Preston held out a hand to stop Finn before he followed her and leaned in to whisper, "Take good care of her. I have a feeling she's something special."

Finn stared into the Minotaur's eyes for a second. "I thought the same thing."

"'The intuition of a dwarf is not something easily questioned,' at least that's what my father always said."

"Sounds like he and I would have gotten along."

Preston chuckled. "I don't know. He was an odd one, my father. Always wore cowboy boots and hats. Huge fan of Marion Robert Morrison, like a superfan. Ended up buying every piece of memorabilia he could find. Made me promise to keep it all after he died. Now I have a whole wing of the house full of the stuff, just collecting dust."

Finn frowned. He had no idea what Preston was talking about, but being a superfan of a guy named Marion did sound odd. How badass could he be?

"Okay. Well, we're off, then." Finn gave him a smile and

walked out the door. He looked at Penny on his shoulder and raised an eyebrow. "Who the fuck is Marion Robert Morrison?"

She turned a little red and gave a stiff shrug, trying not to laugh.

Finn narrowed his eyes at her. He had spent enough time with her to tell when she was lying.

Before he could call her on it, though, Mila shouted for him to hurry up.

CHAPTER TWENTY-THREE

Mila drove them back toward Polo Club, her foot a little less heavy than normal, her fidgeting a sign that she was thinking about everything that could go wrong.

Finn reached over and placed a hand on her leg. "You don't have to do this, you know. You don't owe the magical community anything."

She turned and gave him a hard stare. "I *do* need to do this. For a lot of reasons, but mostly because now that I know there *is* a magical community, I have an obligation to help, out of common decency. In school, Dr. Hoffensteffer always said that to know of a problem and do nothing about it was the most egregious affront to modern civilization. I took that to heart."

Finn squeezed her leg slightly in solidarity. "What are the other reasons?"

She gave a nonchalant shrug. "I told you I was in all the way. I wasn't lying." She smiled at him. "I want to see this to the end. The fact that there is an entire world of magic I get to learn about is better than a thousand new Star Wars movies. I'm having fun with you and Penny. even if that fun sometimes puts holes in my shirts." She chuckled, then sobered before continuing, "Plus, there is something deep inside of me that just feels right about all this. Like it's fate or something."

Finn gave Penny a cocky grin. "Fate? I like the sound of that."

Penny rolled her eyes but didn't comment.

Mila changed the subject. "Okay, we need a better plan than 'get in there and see what's happening.' Any suggestions?"

If there was one thing Finn liked about Mila and needed help with himself, it was that she always wanted a plan. Not that he always gave her one, but the fact that she wanted one at least made him think twice most times.

"How are you with a rifle?" he asked.

"Decent. I grew up in Colorado and Idaho. You can't spend much time in either place without going hunting at least a few times, but I wouldn't say I'm a crack shot or anything."

"Well, it sounds like you're better than me. I think I've shot a gun maybe once, and it wasn't on purpose." He gave her jazz hands. "These are all the projectiles I've ever needed."

She laughed. "That, and you know how to throw Fragar pretty well. Sometime, I'm also going to have to hear the story about you accidentally using a gun, but for now, I'll take the rifle. Does that mean I'll be sitting back a ways?" She took the exit from the freeway and slowed to a stop at the light.

"Can't have you too far back, because we don't know exactly where the hounds will be. Once we find the hounds, you can start dropping them. Hopefully, it will cause enough confusion that I'll be able to get whoever is in charge separated from the group and have a word with them." Finn glanced at Penny. "I think you should stay with Mila. She's going to need the cover more than me."

Penny nodded and gave Mila a thumbs-up.

"Thanks." Mila held out a fist. "It'll be nice to have a friend watching my back."

Penny bumped the offered fist. "Chi." A small smoke ring puffed from a nostril.

"Now, what to do about parking?" Finn thought about the fact that it was a private neighborhood, and there was a security patrol on the lookout for strangers and concluded that street parking was not an option.

"Actually, I have an idea for that." Mila smiled. "Did you notice the huge place under construction down the street from the estate? I think it was backed up against the estate's grounds. We could park there and come in from the rear. Two birds, one stone."

Finn frowned. "What do birds have to do with this?"

Mila rolled her eyes. "You're adorable."

They turned into the lot for the construction site and rolled over the gravel and dirt where the driveway would one day be. The house was little more than a frame, but still impressive due to its sheer size. Mila pulled the Hellcat around back so they would not be visible from the road, and shut the car engine off, killing the headlights.

"I can see the wall from here," Finn said, his dark vision compensating. "Good call, coming here. It's perfect."

"I do what I can." She smiled and climbed out of the driver's seat.

They took a minute while Mila familiarized herself with the rifle. It was magical in construction but had all the same external parts as the hunting rifles she was used to. The only difference was that this one had a small, auto-feed magazine instead of the bolt action she had used years ago. The tranquilizer darts looked mean, with a cylinder full of clear liquid between the black fletching on the back and the two-inch metal spike on the front. She had four magazines with ten rounds each.

Resting the long gun on her shoulder, she gave Finn a nod. "Ready when you are."

He almost laughed at the sight of her four-ten frame holding a gun nearly as long as her body but resisted the urge. "Come on, I can get us inside the wall, but we'll have to move quickly after that. Penny, can you do some scouting before we go in? Keep up high, like last time, and meet us over there when you're done."

Penny gave him a sarcastic salute. "Shiri!" She hopped off his shoulder and flapped into the air, quickly disappearing into the dark, moonless sky.

Finn led Mila through some bushes at the rear of the property, coming out of the underbrush up against a ten-foot, white, stone wall. He held out a hand and focused on the wall itself, trying to feel for any kind of magical alarms, but after a few seconds, determined it was just a stone wall.

He sat down, resting his back against it, and patted the ground beside him. "Take a seat. Penny will be a few minutes, and there's no sense in being nervous until she gets back." He pulled out the box of chews and shook it at her. "Want one?"

She leaned the rifle against the wall and dropped the satchel holding the spare ammo next to it before sitting cross-legged and holding out her hand. "Sure. Why not?"

He shook a few candies into her open hand. "I thought you didn't like these?"

She shrugged, tossing one into her mouth. "They're not my favorite. But why do you always ask if I want some if you thought I didn't like them?"

"Just being polite." He smiled and ate a small handful.

They sat in silence for a few minutes, munching on chocolatey nougat, and waiting for Penny to return.

Mila scooted closer to Finn and leaned against him. "It's a little chilly, just sitting here. I should have worn my hiking gear." She reached up and hugged his arm for warmth.

"Don't worry. Your blood will be pumping soon enough."

"What are you planning on doing with the second condo?" she asked, pulling his arm in tight against her body and shivering slightly.

Finn slipped the box of candies into his coat pocket and reached over to rub some warmth into her leg, his hand sliding over it easily, and building up a good amount of friction on her black fleece leggings. She smiled and nuzzled into his jacket's arm, covering her nose with the leather sleeve.

"Well, I haven't seen the place just yet, but I imagine it's similar to yours. I was going to turn the main room into a workout room so I can teach you how to fight better than to just react like you do now."

She playfully smacked his arm.

"What? It's true. I cringe at the thought of how many times you weren't injured simply because of luck. I'm not knocking your willingness to fight, you have the guts of a dwarf, but you need to know what you're doing. A good offense is the best defense most of the time."

She relented with a nod, not taking her nose off his sleeve, her voice muffled as it came through the leather. "I can see that. It would be nice to know what I'm doing. I feel like a liability half the time."

He patted her leg before continuing to rub it. "You're definitely not a liability. I've lost track of how many times you've saved my ass. I just want you to be safe."

"What else are you thinking about doing, besides the gym?"

"Well, obviously a room for me, and probably one for Penny as well. Now that we have the space, I think she would like a little privacy. But for sure, I'm going to put a hot tub out on the balcony. I love a good, hot soak after a fight."

Finn felt Mila smile against his arm. "A hot tub would be awesome. Maybe even a fire pit, one of the gas ones, so we can go outside even when it's a little chilly."

"I think that's the cold talking, but I like the idea. The balcony view is great, and I would like to enjoy it more," he agreed.

They sat in silence for a few more seconds before Mila

spoke again, her voice barely above a whisper. "I'm glad you're not leaving the condo." She pulled his arm in tight in more of a hug than to fight off the chill.

Finn opened his mouth but couldn't think of anything to say. He finally settled on, "Me too."

Further conversation was cut off when Penny dropped from the sky right in front of them, flapping her wings once before landing. She quickly found a small stick and cleared an area of dirt, then used the stick to sketch the estate—almost exactly to scale, from what Finn could tell.

"I can't see any of that," Mila said, squinting and leaning forward as Penny worked.

"You can't?" Finn asked, cocking his head to the side.

She gave him an *are you kidding me?* face. "It's a moonless night, and we're in a bunch of bushes."

"Oh, right. You don't have dark vision. How did you Peabrains ever survive?" he teased.

Penny finished the drawing and chirped for Mila to wait. She scurried into the brush, twigs snapping quietly, followed by a ripping sound. Penny reemerged with a short stick, one end wrapped in moss and leaves. She breathed a small jet of flame to light the small torch. It sputtered and flickered before settling into a cheery flame that made their shadows dance against the white stone wall.

"Thanks, Penny." Mila was impressed and reached out to take the torch.

"Shir." Penny waved off the comment and turned to the map. She began pointing at buildings and drives, giving a long and complicated series of toots and bursts of flame.

Finn nodded along, translating for Mila as Penny explained what she had seen.

"Evidently, they don't have many wards up yet, and the ones they did have, Penny disabled. She says they were hasty and weak, probably not the permanent ones that need to be etched into stone."

Penny pointed at the main house, and Finn continued.

"The house seems to be more of a barracks and a head-quarters than a proper house. She could see beds and computers set up through almost every window she could get an angle to see through. She counted two dozen Kashgar and says our orc buddies from earlier weren't joking about having a job if they wanted it, because there are twenty orcs out there as well. The patrols are mostly around the house, but if we come through the wall right where we are, and you can tranquilize the guard over here," he pointed to a place on the map that was furthest from the main gate, "then we can get right up to this staging area. They are relying heavily on their wards to warn them if anyone comes in from the back of the property."

"Wait, there are over *forty* guys in there? How the hell are we supposed to fight that?" Mila paled a little in the flickering flame.

"We don't. Ideally, we'll be in and out, then wait for Preston's strike force to get here."

"Shirir! Chi she." Penny pointed to a spot to the right of the back of the house.

"Seriously? Why didn't you say that from the beginning?" Finn grumbled.

Penny shrugged, dipping her head a little with embarrassment. "Chi chi?"

"You were getting to it?" Finn sighed, turning to Mila. "She said the hounds are out in an open pen, but that as she was leaving, a box truck was backing up to it. It looks like they're moving the hounds right now. The good news is that she thinks she found the one who's controlling them. Some big guy in a hooded coat."

Mila brightened up immediately. "That's the guy whose car we followed."

"Shit. We don't have time to wait for the strike team. We have to go in now, and we at least need to take out the leader so they can't control the hounds. Might buy us some time."

"And how are we going to do that?" Mila asked.

Penny pointed at the rifle behind her.

Mila glanced over her shoulder at the gun. "Oh. Fuck."

"We need to move before they can load up the hounds. Take this just in case." He handed her the stone skin ring.

She reached out and took the golden ring, holding it close to the torch to get a better look at it. "I thought you gave this back to Preston?"

He held up his hands in a mini shrug. "I kind of forgot to, after the attack. We can give it to him after this is all done. Now, when you slip it on, it'll take a second or two to activate, but the change happens fairly quickly. This is the most important part, however...you can't wear it for too long."

"Why not?" She cocked her head to the side. "The hound wore it for months, and nothing happened to it."

"That's because hellhounds are magical creatures. The ring can feed off of them to power itself. It was why the poor thing was so hungry when we found her." He tapped a finger lightly against her head. "But you Peabrains turned off that connection to magic. So, if the ring runs out of power, and it tries to feed off of you, you don't have anything to give. At best, it will just stop working, but at worst, it could do some damage to you. I charged it up with my own magic as best I could, but you'll still only have about twenty minutes. It's more of a last resort kind of thing."

She stared at the ring, then put it in one her leggings pockets, its shape visible under the tight fabric. "Okay. I won't use it unless I need to. How tough will it make me?"

"Pretty tough." Finn gave her a stern look. "But it won't make you invulnerable. If you take too much damage with the ring on, you could shatter. Are you ready?"

She gulped and nodded. "Yup. Let's do this."

He pressed his hand to the stone wall and focused his power on the rocks inside it. He heard Mila give a little gasp as his eyes went from brown to light gray, and he began to glow with a purple haze.

Penny, knowing what he was doing, quickly smothered the torch so the light wouldn't give them away.

A circle three feet in diameter began to glow as Finn directed power into the wall. He closed his eyes and visualized what he wanted the stone to do. It was a pretty basic spell, but it took a lot of energy and time to make happen. For nearly two minutes, he focused on the stones with no apparent effect. Then, in a sudden culmination of magic and will, the purple glow vanished, and where it had been solid stone a moment before, fine-grained sand fell to the ground, spilling out from the wall.

What was left was a perfectly circular hole they could easily step through.

"Shit," Mila whispered, picking up a handful of sand

and letting it flow between her fingers. "That was impressive."

"Wait till you see what I can really do," he said with a smile. "Come on. We have to move."

Mila looked at Penny. "Is he just being cocky?"

Penny considered, then waggled her hand back and forth. "Chi shee."

CHAPTER TWENTY-FOUR

Finn kept low, hugging the wall as he made his way around the perimeter. He could hear as Mila padded through the grass close behind him, whispering curses about the darkness. He glanced to the right and could see the estate lit up with outdoor lighting, putting several guards in silhouette as they walked the grounds. He could also see several more people through the windows of the house.

This was really not a fight the three of them wanted to get into, but they needed to stop the hounds from being taken, or they would lose them for good.

They continued moving for what felt like a quarter mile before Finn was able to see the large outdoor pen that Penny had told them about. The barking of the hounds had been present ever since they had crossed onto the property, but now that they had a line of sight, the volume picked up. A few yards from the back of the pen, Finn saw a crop of older trees that would provide them with some cover and perhaps a spot for Mila to be able to shoot from with an unobstructed view.

He paused long enough for Mila to catch her breath. When she gave him a thumbs-up, he pointed to the trees. She nodded, adjusting the satchel of darts on her shoulder. Finn scanned the area and tapped Penny on the shoulder where she crouched in the grass beside him.

She glanced up at him, and he again pointed to the trees, then made a circling motion with his finger. She nodded, and after a few galloping leaps, took off to fly a foot or two over the grass, scouting the area.

Finn crouched down, the low, decorative shrubbery close to the wall covering them from view. Mila held the long rifle in both hands, her eyes wide in the dark as she glanced at the house, then over toward the pen.

"You doing okay?" he asked, leaning in to keep his voice down. "You still cold?"

She chuckled softly. "No, not cold. My blood's going pretty well now, you were right. I'm having trouble seeing, though. I don't know how much help I can be if I can't pick out targets."

Finn considered that, looking at the house and guards. "Well, you'll just have to use the silhouettes, I guess. Though the pen and area around it are lit up pretty well. Plus, if we can get into the trees over there, you'll only be shooting a dozen yards or so. Even I know that's a pretty easy shot." He smiled, but she just nodded, focusing on the trees.

"I can't see much from here, but it looks like it'll be easier from there. That tree has some nice flat branches." She squinted. "I think."

Penny came skimming across the ground and touched down, jogging the last few steps to stop herself. "Chi. Squee cheer."

"That copse of trees is clear and has clear views of the grounds beside the house and down the back drive. We need to hurry, though. She said the truck is backing up to the loading area of the pens now."

As if to prove his point, the sound of beeping filtered over the hounds' barking, and they could see the lights of a large box truck backing into view.

"Let's move while everyone is watching the truck and hearing the hounds," Finn suggested before taking off at a quick, low sprint.

He could hear Mila right behind him as they circled around to the optimal angle. Then Finn turned and parted a couple of bushes and took a quick look. The crop of trees was right in front of them. He could see that the truck was almost in position. He waved for Mila to follow, and sprinted the fifty yards to the trees, trying to keep low, but also trying to get there fast.

The thicket of trees was mostly evergreens, but there were a couple of large oaks in the middle, with vibrant yellow and red leaves still clinging to the branches. Finn dove through two evergreen bushes and found himself in a clearing that hid what looked like a small shed containing gardening equipment.

Mila stumbled to a stop next to him. "I didn't expect to find stuff in here," she whispered between breaths. "Man, I need to do more cardio." She sucked in a deep breath, leaning forward and resting the rifle on her knees.

Finn scanned the clearing, appreciating the use of

space. The two large oaks provided a large area under their branches where the gardeners kept their equipment for the grounds, and the whole mess was hidden by decorative rows of evergreen trees and bushes that surrounded the oaks.

"Are those fireflies, or am I seeing stars from the blood rushing to my head?" Mila said, her head cocked to the side, as she was still bent at the waist, recovering from the sprint.

Finn turned and saw several lightning bugs lazily flashing around the shed. "No, I see them too."

"That's really weird. It's too cold for them to be out." She stood and took one last deep breath. "Anyway, where should I be?"

Finn gestured to the shed. "The roof would give you plenty of space to lay down, and it's tall enough to see over most of the bushes."

She nodded, and Finn stepped to the shed, putting his back to the side and cupping his hands into a stirrup.

"Up you go."

Mila smiled and, holding the gun in one hand, put the other on his shoulder and stepped into his hands. After a second's hesitation, she leaned down and gave him a quick kiss on the lips.

His eyes widened. "What was that for?"

"Luck?" She smiled, then patted his shoulder. "Okay, I'm ready."

"Luck. That works for me." He chuckled. Then, in one smooth motion, he tossed her up onto the roof.

For the first time since she was an undergrad, Mila was thankful she had been on the cheerleading squad in high school and through college. Being as small as she was, she had been what's called a flyer. Flyers are the girls being tossed thirty feet into the air to do the splits before they'd plummet and have to trust that the college dude, who had more than likely been drinking too much the night before and was hungover-but-not-a-quitter, would catch her.

All those years had prepared her for when Finn tossed her the twelve feet up onto the shed's roof.

She only had to windmill with one arm to keep her balance before Penny flew up and pushed her forward onto more solid footing.

"Thanks," Mila breathed to the dragon, who gave her a nod.

She looked back down to see Finn posing a questioning thumbs-up. She gave him an 'OK' sign, and he turned to jog over to the bushes closest to the pen.

Mila laid down and army-crawled to the edge of the roof to look for their target. Penny crawled up and laid beside her, giving the situation her own look.

Mila was relieved to see there was more light around the pens, but there was not nearly as much as she would have liked. She could pick out several pairs of guards, some Kashgar and some Orc, paired by race, looking on as the truck finished backing up to the large chain link pen. For the first time, she was able to see the hounds.

She did a quick count and estimated there to be around twenty-five hounds in total. She marveled that one hellhound had given birth to all of the beasts, less than two months ago.

They were all full-grown and shining with smooth, stone skin of all colors. Some were white, some black, and every geological color in between. Unlike their mother, these hounds didn't seem to have fur and instead were smooth-bodied. She wondered if that was a side effect of the circumstance of their birth, or if it was because their fur wouldn't come until later in life, like how birds had several stages of feathers before adulthood.

Mila pulled up her rifle and began scanning people through the scope. She quickly went through everyone standing in the light but didn't see the one in the hooded jacket.

"Penny," she whispered. "I can't find the guy in charge. Do you see him anywhere?"

"Chi." Penny pointed to the right, and then her eyes went wide. "Shir."

Mila tried to penetrate the darkness, but her human eyes just couldn't do it. Then she saw him walking out of the darkness, right toward the crops of trees they were hiding in. He wasn't alone, and he was gesturing agitatedly at his companion.

As they got closer, Mila could make out that the second man was a tall, blond Kashgar man in a black jacket and dark jeans. His brow was furrowed as he listened to the hooded figure next to him.

The men kept walking closer, obviously trying to get some distance from the hounds so they could talk easier. They stopped right up against the bushes she was sure Finn was hiding in before she could make out their words.

"I don't like this at all, Fredrick," the hooded figure said, his voice angry. "The Selkies were one thing. We needed to know the capabilities of this thing." He shook a golden circlet in one hand. "But if it taught us anything, it's that we need more time to master the control."

Fredrick didn't seem moved. "Mistress has given her orders. The Wooden Bard is a Magical gathering place. Attacking it will make the community demand protection, and we both know there will be none coming for the sake of keeping the community secret from the Peabrains. This gives the movement fuel to gather followers. What can be safer than a country of their own, with their best interests at heart, and not those of the willfully blind Peabrains?"

"I understand the concept, but The Wooden Bard is not exclusively frequented by Magicals. There will be Peabrains there as well, which means the police will be called. We are not established enough to subvert police yet. Why not pick a place like one of the markets or another Magical-exclusive location? We could control the outcome better."

Fredrick sighed as if he had explained this a thousand times before. "Because if the attack is on a place only Magicals know exists, then it would have to have been perpetrated by a Magical. By picking a target that is well known even to the Peabrains who are in the know about Magicals, then we can build the narrative that it's a Peabrain hate group. We have been over this. If you can't perform your duties to the mistress, then we can find someone who can."

The hooded figure waved off the threat with a contemptuous hand. "Don't give me that doom and gloom shit, Fredrick. You know as well as I do that you can't replace me without a lot of trouble. I was personally asked to join by the mistress. Can you say that?"

Fredrick set his jaw. "The word of the mistress is law. You know that."

"I do, but I still think it's a mistake to move so quickly. Especially with Dr. Winters and that fucking dwarf sniffing around. Our man said he was taking care of him, but I'll believe that when I see his bearded head on a spike, and not a second before. Dwarves are dangerous beyond anything you goddamned assholes want to believe, but what do I know? I've only studied them my *entire life*."

"Are you going to complete the raid, or am I going to have to call the mistress in to deal with you?" Fredrick was glowering but kept from shouting.

"I'm working on it."

The hooded man turned his back to Mila and faced the pens with the hounds; Fredrick turned his back to her as well to watch.

The first man lowered his hood, but all Mila could see was a head of thick, black hair. With a deliberately slow movement, he lowered the circlet onto his head with two hands, twitching slightly, as if a shock of pain had shot through him. She could see the circlet begin to glow with a purple light before he lifted the hood back in to place.

Mila saw movement from below as Finn parted the bushes and stepped out behind the two men. He glanced up at her, making a finger gun at the hooded figure, then he pulled Fragar out and stepped up behind the Kashgar. He raised the axe's handle with one hand, then lifted the other, holding up three fingers. He slowly lowered the first finger.

Mila's heart jumped in her throat as she realized he was counting down the attack.

She quickly aimed the rifle at the hooded man's back. The sound of howling and barking intensified as the hounds went wild. She glanced down and saw Finn's second finger drop.

The hooded man raised a hand, his fingers splayed, then closed it into a fist.

The hounds fell silent and stood as still as statues.

The sound of Fragar unfolding was plain as day in the sudden silence, making the Kashgar spin around and find Finn looming behind him.

"Fire!" Finn shouted, slamming the flat of his axe into Fredrick's face and knocking the man out cold.

Mila pulled the trigger. The magical rifle bucked in her hands, but there was no loud *crack* of gunpowder, only the *whoosh* of the dart shooting out of the barrel, and the *thwack* of it hitting the hooded man in the shoulder.

He stumbled forward, falling to a knee. Fredrick crumpled to the ground beside him.

The hounds went wild once again as he lost control, the animals snarling with even more anger and determination than before. Many of the guards ventured closer to the pens while looking around for the problem.

The man lowered his hood and turned angry, black eyes on Finn. He bared his teeth below his long, pointed nose, the short, greenish fur on his neck rising slightly, like a cat hissing at its prey.

Mila realized he wasn't an Orc at all. He was a Troll. And he looked familiar.

The tranq dart should have put him down, but he didn't seem to be getting tired at all. She lined up another shot, and the *whoosh-thwap* of another dart hitting home seemed to enrage him even more as he turned and spotted Mila on the roof.

She saw his eyes soften before he turned and ran.

"Intruders! In the trees!"

His roaring voice carried over the snarling hounds and attracted the attention of every guard in the area.

CHAPTER TWENTY-FIVE

Mila watched Finn start after the troll, but he stopped a few steps in, turning back to Mila, considering what to do.

"Shoot as many guards as you can. We need to get out of here," he shouted before charging the closest guard coming at him.

Mila glanced at Penny, who had a worried look on her face but gave her a sharp nod, obviously wanting to take off, but she stayed put for some reason. Mila tried her best, firing three shots before Finn met with the first guard and punched him full in the face, never stopping his full out sprint. The guard was slammed into the grass and didn't move after Finn was gone. Mila tried her best to hit the guards that were slowly circling around him, but it was too dark to pick them out once they left the light. She wasn't even sure she had hit one of them.

She could see that Finn was leading them out into the open of the back yard of the estate. He wasn't sticking around long enough to get into any long exchanges that she could see. Instead, he would land a blow then move, making the growing group of Kashgar and Orcs have to reposition after each attack. However, they were closing the circle slowly.

Mila had to roll up into a sitting position as he led them further back into the estate's yard. The gun clicked, and she pulled the trigger again, and again it clicked empty. Penny tapped her knee with a fresh magazine.

"I don't know if I'm doing any good here. I can't see the targets for shit in the dark." Mila complained as she dropped the used mag and slammed a new one in. She glanced down, looking for the slide to chamber a round, forgetting the gun was magical and didn't have any mechanical parts. Sitting on the stock next to her hand was a lightning bug, lazily flashing with green light.

An idea struck Mila. She had never really tried to ask an insect for anything more complicated than to leave or not bother her friends, but they seemed to be much more responsive lately. She decided to take a chance. If it didn't work, then it wouldn't make things any worse than they already were.

She leaned forward, lifting the bug closer to her. "Hey there, little man. You think you and your friends could do me a huge favor?"

Finn kicked an orc in the nuts, lifting the seven-foot bastard off the ground a good foot and a half. The orc's high-pitched scream was music to Finn's ears.

He was doing his best to keep the rage from taking

hold, but he was having trouble dealing with all the opponents without the increased reaction time his berserker state bestowed upon him. While the rage had its advantages, especially in a fight with multiple people, it had one major drawback so significant that he had been deemed unfit to join the royal guard for the customary stint as his ancestors had before him.

While he was in a rage, he was tougher and faster, but utterly unable to cast any type of spell. The rage itself was like an anti-magic serum. Not only was it impossible for him to cast anything, but magic used against him became less potent the further the rage had taken him.

Right now, he needed to have a clear mind for what was coming next.

There were at least two dozen Orcs and Kashgar surrounding him, most of whom had a weapon of some kind. He fought them off as best he could, but he was starting to gather a small collection of cuts and bruises. He needed them to come in closer.

In truth, he needed Mila to start hitting some goddamned people with that big ass rifle. He kept forgetting that she couldn't see in the dark the way he and Penny could, but he felt like the law of averages said she should be hitting something, even if it was blind luck.

As if his prayers were being answered, the Kashgar coming at him with a collapsible baton was hit in the chest by a tranq dart that spun the large man around and sprawling on the grass, completely knocked out in the fraction of a second it took to fall.

Finn suddenly had the thought that she might accidentally hit him in the dark, but quickly decided that was not the way an epic story should go, and fate surely had other plans for him.

Finn kicked the legs out from under an Orc before taking a glancing blow to the ear from behind. He spun to find a Kashgar off balance from the swing, but several more of his fellows were closing in behind him.

Suddenly a green light lit up the chest of the man in front of him. A second later, the *thwap* of a dart hitting him in the chest right next to the light made Finn's eyes widen. The lightning bug took off and found an Orc, landing on his shoulder. A second later and other dart hit the orc in the shoulder.

Finn blocked a baton strike with the flat of Fragar before cutting off a hand that got a little too close. *Thwap! Thwap!* Two more went down. It didn't seem to matter if they were Orc or Kashgar, the darts took them down nearly instantly, the potent tranquilizer as effective as Anita promised.

The numbers were still too thick for Mila to take them all out, but it was enough that the stragglers were able to close in on Finn, tightening their circle and landing more and more blows.

It was time.

Finn crouched down, covering his head with his arms to protect himself for the duration of the spell. The entire time he had been fighting the guards off and drawing them in at the same time he had been constructing a spell in the back of his head, drawing magic from the ground to power the construct in his head. It was a spell he had learned during his time with his tutors back at his father's palace. He had never used the spell before, for the simple reason that he had never had anyone with him that could deal with the aftermath.

Finn hoped Penny could explain what he was about to do and that Mila would be able to get them out of there afterward.

He trusted them. Now he just needed to trust in the magic that was quickly filling him to the bursting point.

Mila smiled as she saw the next firefly light up a target. She pulled the trigger, and the green bioluminescent glow faded as the target fell. Then another lit up, and another target went down in a heap.

Penny tapped her arm with a fresh magazine, and Mila quickly changed it out for the spent one. She saw Finn crouched in the middle of the close grouping of enemies, his outline glowing purple with magical energies.

"What is he doing?" she pointed out Finn to Penny, who frowned, smoke pouring from her in worry. "He's going to get himself killed, not fighting back."

Mila started to get up to help, but Penny put a hand on her knee. "Shir. Chi chi." She mimed using the rifle.

Mila hesitated for a second, then pressed the stock to her shoulder and took another series of shots, every other shot she would check on Finn. His glow was brighter, so much so that she could now see the area immediately around him shrouded in purple light. She could now see several batons connect against his arms as he protected himself. She sighted in on the offending baton wielders and put a dart into each of them, but they were replaced instantly by more coming in behind them.

The grouping was now just a tight pack of people beating Finn down. Mila wanted to scream, but she didn't see that it would do any good. Instead, she emptied the second clip, but there were still almost thirty guards packed in around Finn.

The rifle clicked empty once again, but when she held out a hand to Penny for the last magazine, the small dragon wasn't paying attention.

"Hey." Mila nudged Penny with her knee, but Penny just pointed at Finn, then clasped her hands in worry.

Mila watched the purple light quickly grow in intensity until it was difficult to look at Finn directly. The group around him finally seemed to understand that they had not trapped him; he had been the one setting the trap.

Several of the Kashgar, being a little quicker on the uptake, turned and began to run, but it was too late.

The light glaring off of Finn suddenly shrunk down to a pinpoint centered in his chest. There was a breathless moment when the night stood still, Mila's eyes widening in the sudden darkness before the night was lit like a noonday sun, Finn at its center.

Mila had to look away from the intensity as her eyes adjusted, but Penny never turned her head, just squinting, wanting to watch the entire spell.

A ripping sound filled the night, like a mix between an avalanche and a hundred trees being ripped in half. Screams filled the night and cut off, followed by the sounds of dozens of bodies hitting the ground. The earth rumbled and shook, nearly tipping Mila from the shed's roof.

Penny put a hand on Mila's knee, steadying herself with one hand and punching the air with the other. "Shi!" she cheered, shooting a victory flame into the night sky.

Mila was still trying to recover what small amount of night vision she had, but the sound of a truck rumbling to life made her glance at the pens and the small island of light they had. In the mad dash of trying to hit as many targets as she could, she failed to notice the hounds quieting down and finally falling silent. She expected to find them standing in their pens, but the chain-link fences were empty, the hounds having been loaded into the box truck during the fight. The truck lights came on and it lurched into gear, rocking from side to side as it rumbled down the back drive and through the gate.

Mila turned back to squint into the darkness, trying to pick Finn out. Her eyes adjusted just enough to see the ragged outline of things sticking out of the ground at odd angles encircling the spot where Finn had been.

"Chi! Shee, cheer!" Penny tugged on her sleeve, pulling her towards the edge of the roof.

Mila got the message and slung the rifle over her shoulder along with the satchel of magazines. She scooted to the edge on her butt, the asphalt tiles catching on her leggings and breaking small bits of grit loose to tumble down the gabled roof. She scooted to the edge and launched herself off, landing in a crouch, and sprinted after Penny, who had already swooped past her and through the evergreen bushes.

She came bursting out of the coverage and stumbled on a rock that was lying in the grass. She caught herself but noticed there were several more large stones scattered in the neatly trimmed grass. Having to slow her run gave Mila the opportunity to survey the damage better.

There were Orcs and Kashgar strewn all across the yard, some nearly a hundred feet from the epicenter that had been Finn. Most of them were out cold, or dead, she couldn't tell as she ran past them in the dark, but a few groaned with obviously broken arms or legs.

Penny called out, making Mila look up from a particularly mangled Orc. She skidded to a halt, nearly running into an outcropping of rock, black soil clinging to its tip where it had been shoved through the soil violently. She glanced around her in amazement. Several dozen such outcroppings jutted out of the ground in an angle away from the center. She guessed there had to be several hundred tons of rock that had come from the earth. It was as if Stonehenge had been weaponized.

"Chi!" Mila heard Penny shout from further in the stone formation.

Mila picked her way through, finding row after row of the stone to finally enter a perfectly circular area of bare ground. Finn lay on his back, his eyes still gray and a half-drunk smile on his face.

"Chi chi!" Penny pulled on Finn's hand, barely moving it, but looking up at Mila.

"How am I supposed to move him? He's like four times my weight!" Mila squatted down next to him and lightly slapped his face. "Come on, big guy. We need to get out of here. Wake up!"

Finn's head rolled her way, his heavy-lidded eyes half-focusing on her. "Yer pretty." He giggled.

"What the fuck is wrong with him?" Mila asked Penny, her brow furrowing.

Penny frowned then crouched, shaking her hands over her head, miming a big explosion along with the sound effects. She stood up quickly. "SHOOSH!" She then stumbled around, miming being drunk, and fell over backward.

"Oh, the spell made him drunk?"

Penny looked up from her back and wobbled her hand in a "sort of" motion.

"I still can't lift him." Mila pulled on his hand, barely moving him.

Penny launched herself at Mila, wrapping around her leg and tapping furiously at the outline of the ring in the pocket of Mila's leggings.

Mila pulled the gold ring out and regarded it skeptically. "Will this make me stronger?"

Penny nodded, climbing up onto her shoulder.

Mila slipped the ring on, bracing for what was coming next. She relaxed after a few seconds when nothing happened. "Is it supposed…"

A cold chill ran through her, and her jaw clenched shut. She squeezed her eyes closed and made her hands into fists as the chill went all the way through her down to the bone. Her teeth would have chattered with the chill, but she couldn't move in the slightest as the spell took hold and transformed her into a living statue.

CHAPTER TWENTY-SIX

Finn hadn't felt this good and drunk in a long time. Usually, it took him several bottles of whiskey before he felt even the slightest of buzzes but using that much magic all at once was a sure way to put his body into a stupor.

He was aware that he had completed the spell, calling on the rocks to protect him, and he knew it had worked, but after that, things were a little more nebulous.

He knew he was in a vehicle, and that that vehicle was barreling down the road, but he didn't remember getting into the car at all. In fact, the only thing he remembered was the ivory face of an angel looking down at him and smiling. Then a brief memory of being carried over someone's shoulder. He had thought at the time that they must be short because his hands were dragging in the grass, but the feel of the cool blades of green had felt so good against his skin that he forgot to ask about their height.

There was something he was supposed to be doing, but

he couldn't focus, and the seat he was reclined in was so comfortable.

A small face full of teeth and leaking smoke from its nostrils leaned in to fill his vision. "Squee. Squee!" two small hands grabbed a handful of his beard and shook his face.

He knew that face. "Pen?" he mumbled, words not coming easily.

The head bobbed up and down. "Chi! Squee."

"Is he going to be all right?" a delightful female voice asked.

Finn rolled his heavy head to the side and saw a long-haired beauty sitting next to him in the driver's seat. He knew her too. How could he ever forget a face like that?

"Mi. So pretty." His hand flopped over to land on her thigh as he tried to pat it, but it was too heavy for him to pick up again. "Sorry bout 'iss."

She laughed. "You're not the first drunk guy I've had to take care of."

He frowned then shook his head. "No. Sorry 'bout needen oo. Should be tougher."

Mila went a little still, her mouth flattening out into a line of disapproval. "Don't be sorry that you need help. That's ridiculous. We all need help sometimes." She glanced over, making brief eye contact. "Even if we don't ask for it like we should, sometimes. God knows I'm guilty of it too."

He smiled, his face feeling heavy. "Iss good. Ast why I lurvoo."

He saw her eyes go a little wide as she glanced back at him before turning back to the road and keeping them there. She was silent long enough that he almost fell asleep, but her whispered reply snapped him awake again.

"I don't know if that one counts. You're obviously drunk." She clenched at the steering wheel, her knuckles white.

"Chi?" His head rolled down to find Penny on his lap, but she was looking at Mila, her head cocked and eye ridges raised questioningly.

"What? It's only been like a month!" Mila said, defensively. "This is not the conversation we should be having right now."

Penny rolled her eyes and held up a little white business card. Finn recognized the card but couldn't remember where he had gotten it.

"Oh, right!" Mila seemed embarrassed. "Finn, buddy, I need you to get a message to Hermin. Hermin, you remember? The gnome? We need him to meet us at the Wooden Bard. I can't send the card, and Penny can't communicate with them. We need you to focus. Remember the hounds? We need to stop them."

Finn furrowed his brow, watching her speak. She was so earnest in her need for him to do this. He reached out with a shaky hand and grabbed for the card, but missed, making Penny have to duck under his swinging arm. She hopped onto his forearm as it passed on his second attempt and placed the card in his hand.

He looked at it, forgetting what it was for a second before Mila reached over and squeezed his knee. "Hermin. Get Hermin to the Wooden Bard. We need to stop the hounds."

Finn squinted his eyes in concentration.

Mila changed lanes and hit the gas. She wasn't entirely sure where the Wooden Bard was, but she had entered it into the GPS of her phone and the pleasant British-sounding voice told her that it was only about ten minutes away. After using the ring to move Finn to the car, she had taken a good two minutes to take it off again and return to her normal condition. She figured, with the time it had taken to carry Finn to the car and get him situated, the Troll had already arrived at the bar, and the attack was underway.

Returning to normal after the comfortable chill of her stone skin had been one of the weirdest experiences in her life. It was like growing flesh from nothing in the span of seconds. She shivered, thinking about it.

Glancing over, she saw Finn concentrating, his hand and the card held between his fingers glowing with the barely visible purple light of his magic. He opened his mouth, then closed it, smacking his lips a few times before continuing.

"Wooden Bard." He said the words forcefully, enunciating as best he could. "Hounds. Help." He took a breath, his eyes rolling with effort. "Bring deep stones. Black deep." His head fell back against the headrest and he released the card.

Instead of the glowing card falling to his lap, it was enveloped in a small bubble and vanished with a pop.

Finn smiled, his shoulders slumping, eyes closing, and his breathing becoming deep and steady. The small act of sending the card off seemed to have been just enough to put him over the edge into unconsciousness. Mila squeezed Finn's knee one last time, giving him a thin-lipped smile.

Penny and Mila shared a look. The dragon had a half a cheesy grin on her face. "What?" Mila asked, narrowing her eyes in suspicion.

Penny just glanced down at her hand on Finn's leg then gave her a wink.

"Oh, stop it." She snatched her hand away. "Should we get Danica to come to the bar? Just in case there are a lot of hurt people? She might be able to do a lot of good."

Penny thought about it for a second then nodded, a ring of smoke rising from a nostril in the affirmative. "Shir."

Mila hit the voice control for the car. "Call Danica." The car let off a tone, and the sound of her phone ringing came through the speakers.

"Hello?" Danica's answered after a few rings. "Are you guys okay? It's after ten."

Mila was surprised that it had gotten so late in the day. "We're okay." She glanced at Finn slumped in the seat. "Ish." She amended. "We need your help. There's going to be an attack on the Wooden Bard, and I think we could use your healing arts during the cleanup. Can you meet us there?"

There was the sound of rustling cloth on Danica's side of the call. "Yeah. I can be there in a few minutes. Let me put on some clothes and grab my bag."

"Were you sleeping?" Mila asked, shocked that Danica would be caught dead in bed before midnight. The sound of a man's voice came through, though it was too muffled for Mila to make out the words. "Oh, my god. Is that Phil?" Mila chuckled when she recognized the man's odd tone.

"Maybe. Doesn't matter. We can talk about this later. I'll

be there in a few minutes." Danica hung up before Mila could grill her further.

She grinned at Penny who shared the expression. "Well, looks like our little elf girl is joining the dork side."

Penny rolled her eyes at the pun.

"Mmm, I like yer dork side," Finn mumbled, his eyes cracking open ever so slightly.

Mila chuckled. "Is that so? What about my dork side do you like?"

"Way it feels."

"You like the way my dorkiness feels?" She asked, confused how that made any sense.

Finn rolled his heavy head back and forth in the negative. "Nnnn. Way *you* feel."

She rolled her eyes. "You like the way I feel? And how, exactly, do I feel to you?" she had been hoping for something a little more than talk of her physical body, but it was still nice to hear.

Finn rolled his head her way, his eyes heavily lidded, but she could see the sparkling gray of his magically influenced eyes regard her in all seriousness. "You feel like home."

The words hit her harder than she thought they would have, and she had to swallow a sudden lump in her throat. When she glanced away from the road, she could see that he was out once again, but Penny was looking up at him, her eyes moist. She saw Mila looking and gave her a nod of agreement. She felt the same in her own way.

CHAPTER TWENTY-SEVEN

Mila double-parked in front of the Wooden Bard. Luckily it was on a side street, so there wasn't much traffic that needed to go around her. She was surprised the white box truck wasn't out on the street as well since she didn't think she had been driving fast enough to pass the Troll.

She put on her flashers and leaned over the center console to get a better view of the bar. There were only two windows in the front of the building, one on either side of the glass front door. All three windows were frosted, so the only thing she could pick out was the neon Coors sign hanging in the left window and the fact that the lights were on.

Rolling down the window, Mila could hear music playing and almost thought she was in the wrong place, but a scream cut through the country pop song playing inside, letting her know that the GPS had done its job properly. The front door swung open and a woman stumbled out a few steps before falling to the sidewalk, her leg bleeding through a tight pair of ripped jeans.

Mila's eyes went wide, and she turned to climb out of the car to help the woman. The large-nosed man leaning in, cupping his face against the driver side window, made her scream and reach for Gram. The face jumped back and held up his hands.

"Hermin?" Mila shouted, opening her car door and throwing a crumpled empty box of Charleston Chews Finn had left in the cup holder at him. "You scared the fucking shit out of me! You need to help the girl." She pointed towards the sidewalk.

"Dr. Meadows is taking care of her," Hermin said, handing a leather sack to Mila. "Sorry it took so long. We had to stop and collect her on our way. Here are the stones Finn requested."

Mila turned back and saw Danica pulling the woman away from the door, along with Garret. She had her large sack of healing reagents over her shoulder. A pop made her look farther down, where another Huldu appeared in a large bubble, followed by several more.

"We will be able to keep the Peabrains from getting loose before we can alter their memories, but it's limited, so we need to take care of this quickly," Hermin said, leaning into the car and seeing Finn passed out in the passenger seat. "What the hell happened to him?"

"Used too much magic at once, I think. Penny said it makes dwarves drunk. Or it makes berserkers drunk. Maybe it just makes Finn drunk?" Mila shrugged and held up the sack of stones. "What are these for exactly?"

Hermin shrugged. "He asked for deep stones, so I brought them."

Penny quickly climbed up Mila's back and over her shoulder, grabbing the sack and scurrying back to Finn. To Mila and Hermin's horror, she opened the sack, pulled out a black polished stone, and promptly shoved it down Finn's throat. She was pushing so hard that she had to stand on his chest and use her full weight, pushing the black stone down until she was shoulder-deep down his throat. Withdrawing her saliva-slick arm, she repeated the process with a second stone.

"What the hell are you doing?" Mila asked, her mouth hanging open. "He's going to choke to death."

Penny didn't seem to notice Mila's shouting, instead shoving a third black stone down Finn's throat. She was so determined and seemed to know what she was doing, so Mila just sat there watching until the bag was empty, and Penny was wiping the saliva from her arm with the front of Finn's black t-shirt. She then turned to Mila and held up one taloned finger.

"One minute?" Mila guessed.

Penny nodded and patted Finn on the chest, a smoke ring shooting from a nostril.

Mila climbed out of the car, Hermin giving her a hand. "What should we do? Go in without him?"

Hermin shook his head emphatically. "Not with a bunch of hellhounds loose in there. We would be torn to shreds. Hellhounds are fairly resistant to magic already, but with the stone skin, I can't even imagine magic working on them at all."

"But the troll is using magic to control them." She

mimed putting on a tiara. "He has a crown thing we think is a dwarven artifact. At least, I saw that purple magic light stuff around it that Finn puts off when he uses a spell."

"Aura. The light is called an aura." Danica said, stepping up to them, pulling off a pair of latex gloves covered in blood. "That would explain why it's working on the hounds. Dwarven magic is part of the earth, the ground. It is extremely effective on things like stone."

Mila gave her friend a hug. "Thanks for coming."

"It's my duty to look after the health of my people. Technically it's my duty to look after all people, not just my own. We even had to take an oath about it before we could graduate." She smirked. "Speaking of, why are we not getting in there to stop this attack?"

"We need Finn," Garret said, joining them. "He's the only one who can use magic effectively against the hounds, and it doesn't hurt that he's a hell of a fighter as well."

"Yeah, but he's out cold." Mila leaned down and looked in on him. He was still lying back in the passenger seat as Penny had left him, mouth agape and a line of saliva down his beard.

"What's wrong with him?" Danica asked, her voice rising an octave as she leaned down beside Mila and saw the passed-out man.

"He used too much magic at once? I think."

Penny nodded, keeping her eyes on Finn's face.

Mila opened her mouth to ask when he was going to wake up, but she was cut off by Finn's eyes opening wide, the gray color having gone nearly white in intensity. He leaned forward and coughed hard, even taking one fist and hitting himself hard in the stomach. Blood rushed to his face, turning him crimson before he coughed once again. This time two stones came flying out of his open mouth, and he sucked in a deep breath before coughing up the last four in one go.

To Mila's surprise, the stones were now chalk-white, and brittle. One of the stones had hit the dashboard and split in two, leaving a chalky residue on the black leather.

Finn blinked, wiped tears from his eyes, and looked down at Penny. "Thanks," he croaked.

"Chi! Shir she chi!" She pointed to the bar's front door urgently.

"Shit! We're already here?" He looked around, noticing Mila and Danica staring at him open-mouthed. "Danica? How did… You know what? It doesn't matter. We'll talk after. You ready Mila? Still have the ring?"

Mila pulled the ring from her pocket, still not understanding what had happened. "Yeah. Right here."

"Put it on. It'll protect you from the hounds' bites, but don't get overwhelmed. They have strong jaws, and I wouldn't want you to lose an arm." He pushed the door open and climbed out in one smooth motion, not showing any sign of his previous stupor. He pulled Fragar out, activated the axe, and looked back over his shoulder at Mila. "Let's go to work."

CHAPTER TWENTY-EIGHT

Finn watched as Mila slipped the gold ring on and closed her eyes. Her skin lightened from its normal dark tan coloring to pale, then continued on to the silky ivory color of polished marble. Even her hair, from the roots out, changed to impossibly thin ivory strands that glinted in the streetlights. She gave a shiver before opening her eyes, their rich, vibrant brown cutting through the white marble skin and setting Finn's heart to fluttering.

She looked like a perfect statue that would have made Michelangelo jealous.

A smile formed on her white lips. "What?"

"You look like a Valkyrie." He said, not knowing a better comparison.

"I hope not. I wouldn't want to drag your dead ass all the way to Hel." She laughed.

Finn shrugged. "I don't think I'd mind, as long as it were you doing the dragging."

She rolled her eyes, pulling Gram free and whispering the power word that unfolded the blade. "What's the plan?"

Penny climbed up on Mila's shoulder, unfurling her wings and giving them a flap to loosen up. "Chi! Shir she."

Finn nodded. "What she said; get the circlet off the troll and take him down. Penny and me will do our best to distract the hounds. See if you can find a way to get the people out of there, but if the opportunity presents itself, take him out. We can deal with the wild hounds easier than if they're actively directed to kill us...I hope."

The sound of more screaming filtered out past the country music, making Finn narrow his eyes. "Right. Hermin, Danica, prepare for the injured. Mila, Penny, let's do this."

Finn marched to the front door, pulled it open hard enough that it cracked the glass, and stepped inside. His eyes were narrowed, Fragar held to the side glowing with power, and an aura of danger radiating from his hulking figure.

A cacophony of utter chaos hit him like a wall. The sound of country music playing at a high volume mixed with the screaming of confused and hurt people, along with the snap and crackle of magic, filled the dim interior of the Wooden Bard.

Making room for Mila, Finn surveyed the medium-sized bar. The wooden motif extended further than just the name. Dark paneling covered the walls trimmed in royal red wallpaper around the top. Wooden pillars held up the thick wooden ceiling beams, and booths of solid oak lined the walls.

The long mahogany bar across the back of the room was being used as a kind of battlement by several customers of magical descent. They had formed up, using the thick wooden structure to keep a dozen hellhounds at bay while pelting them with bubbles of magic that burst into flame, or crackled with electricity. One of the casters was obviously well versed in cold magic, leaving jagged patches of ice splashed across floor and hound alike.

Outside of the makeshift barricade was a slaughter field, mostly consisting of non-magicals. Several people were down on the floor, doing their best to fight off the monsters that had come to life from their nightmares. They used whatever was at hand. Stools or chairs seemed to be the most effective, but a solid bite from the stone jaws bit through the wood with little resistance. Almost everyone was bloody, and some were obviously not moving, even when the hounds left them alone and moved on to new targets.

At the center of it all was the Troll, his hood down with his back to them, dark hair pinned to his head by the golden circlet that crackled with raw, purple power. In one hand he held a staff he used as both a club and a casting instrument. Finn watched as he smacked a woman across the face with the end of the staff, before pointing it at a young man, running for the back door, and shooting a thin line of bubbles at him. The bubbles acted as a living rope, wrapping him up and sending him sprawling to the floor where a hound pounced on him and sunk its teeth into his shoulder.

Finn was about to charge into the fray when he saw a stool fly past him and smack into the Troll's shoulder, making him stumble before turning their way.

Finn glanced over and saw the ivory form of Mila, her teeth clenched, another stool in her hands ready to throw.

Her fierce look fell away to be replaced with confusion when the troll locked gazes with her.

"Jeffery?" She took a step closer, the stool raised and ready to throw.

Finn glanced back at the troll and saw that he was using a concealment spell to look like his human form, and Finn was surprised to recognize the man from a photo Mila had shown him of her missing coworker from the museum.

Finn noticed the hounds had stopped attacking for a moment as Mila and Jeffery stared one another down, obviously distracted by their controller's sudden lack of focus.

"Mila. I told you to drop it." Jeffery roared, his face turning dark. "Didn't you get my note? I didn't want you to have anything to do with any of this." There was a tinge of regret in his rage.

"What the hell is all of this, Jeff?" Mila waved a hand that included the hurt people on the ground. "Why would you do this?"

"You wouldn't understand. This is about freedom and having a place to belong." He ground his teeth. "Something you Peabrains enjoy with your willful ignorance."

"Looks more like it's about control and domination to me," Finn remarked, keeping an eye on the semi-docile hounds. Several of the people had been able to crawl away to relative safety, a few even making it out the door behind them, while Mila kept the troll occupied.

Jeffery barked a wicked laugh. "That's rich coming from a dwarf, and a royal one to boot. You people are the definition of domineering."

"Makes it all the easier for me to pick it out when I see

it." He stepped closer, raising an eyebrow. "Mila made it sound like you were a reasonable man. What exactly is it about the goddamned Dark Star that took you in? Power? Prestige? What?"

Jeffery's face grew hard, and he glanced at Mila. "I'm sorry, but you are now in the way. I tried to spare you, but you just wouldn't let it go, would you? Always going just a little too far for your own good."

"You don't have to do this, Jeff." Mila pleaded, her very human eyes misting with tears.

"Yes, I do." He pointed the staff at Mila and sent a series of bubbles racing her way.

Finn shoved her hard, sending her stumbling to the side as the bubbles raced between them to splash across the wall where they burst into flame, curling the wallpaper in a wash of intense heat. Finn threw Fragar right at Jeffery's face, but the troll was faster than Finn had expected and deflected the spinning axe with the end of his staff. Finn didn't let that deter him, as he had followed up the axe with a charge.

He was a step away from getting his hands around Jeffery's throat when several tons of hellhound tackled him from the side. Finn counted four of the giant, heavy beasts fighting to be the first to take a bite out of his face as they hit the ground in a tumbling mess. Focusing a quick spell on the tangle of stone-coated animals, he bound the rock of their skin together where they touched one another, locking all four of them in the tangle they had created of their bodies.

The hounds were still on top of him, but he was at least safe from their teeth. He shoved with all his strength, and with a huge effort was able to roll the mess off of himself, the hounds yelping in fear now that they couldn't move apart.

Finn saw Penny racing around the room, doing her best to distract hounds as they attacked bystanders. She would shoulder-check a hound in the face, letting it snap its teeth at her before drawing it away, staying just out of reach, and lead it recklessly into the side of another hound, sending both beasts tumbling away from another victim.

Mila had three hounds on her, one clamped onto her leg, the cloth of her leggings shredded below the knee but her stone skin showing only minor scratches from its teeth. A second had hold of her left arm at the wrist, keeping Gram out of the fight and trying to pull her off balance while a third snapped at her face. She swung her right fist into the top of the third hound's head, snapping its teeth together with the force of the blow, sending it to the ground where it whined, a small chunk of stone missing from its forehead.

Finn rolled to his feet just in time to be hit in the chest by a series of bubbles from Jeffery's staff, each one bursting into flame, and sending him reeling back into a table and chairs. He smacked at the flames, but before he could properly get them out, a hound tackled him, sending him over the table. He shouted in pain as it bit down on his arm.

Blood splashed across his face from the torn flesh of his arm. He gritted his teeth, punching the hound in the side of its face, knocking it loose from his forearm. Getting a foot under its belly, he shoved it off, quickly regaining his feet just in time for the beast to snap at his arm again. He pulled back, but it just kept coming, leaping at his face.

"Teacht le cheile." Finn held out his hand, glowing with power, and touched the hound on the head as it flew towards him.

There was a flash of purple dwarven magic, and when the hound's feet touched the ground, they continued through the solid stone floor as if it had landed on water. It sank up to its chest, its eyes wide with fear. The spell ran its course and the hound's stone skin fused with the stone flooring, trapping the animal in place.

Finn ignored its whining and sprinted towards Fragar, which was lying beside one of the booths with two people cowering from a hound that was doing its best to climb the table. He snatched the hound's tail, twisting to get some leverage, and flung the huge animal into the center of the room in a yelping tangle.

He grabbed his axe and pointed at the relatively clear path to the front door. "Run! There are people outside waiting to help."

He didn't wait to see if the cowering Peabrains followed his instructions. He rushed close to Jeffery to take a swing at his exposed back.

And was tackled by another hound.

***

Mila finally wrenched the hand holding Gram free from the viselike grip of the hellhound's jaws and backhanded it in the face. The sound of stone smacking against stone cracked over the blaring country music as the hound, knocked senseless, went tumbling to the ground. Gritting her teeth, she swung Gram at the hound still attached to her leg. The golden blade sparked and ricocheted off the beast's neck, but it was enough to knock it loose from her appendage. She wasted no time kicking it hard in the midsection, her stone enhanced body sending the hound tumbling through the air and directly into Finn, who was charging up behind Jeff, Fragar out for the kill.

"Oh, shit! Sorry!" she shouted, sucking in a breath between her teeth.

Jeffery only noticed Finn because of her mistake and turned the full force of his powers on the dwarf.

Mila could see that Penny was doing her best, but she was only one small dragon surrounded by large stone hellhounds. She would breathe fire into their faces, but it was a wholly magical fire, and it had basically no effect on the magic-hardened hounds.

More and more people were escaping as Jeffery had to pull more and more hounds into the fight with them, but there were still a good dozen patrons left, other than the ones too injured to move. They needed to stop this now.

Her finger started to itch, and she glanced down to see that it was sparking slightly, and the skin immediately around the ring was turning dark and had burn marks. She could feel the spell of stone starting to recede from deep within her. She did a quick calculation, and with the time it had taken to get Finn into the car and the fight now, her time was almost up. The ring's power was running out.

She saw Finn struggling to fight off hounds and Jeffery at the same time, and took the opportunity presented. She charged in, snatching up a barstool and throwing it with all her considerable might.

The wooden stool exploded on Jeffery's back, making

him stumble forward and breaking off his attack on Finn. He turned, his face sour with pain and his staff ready for an attack.

Mila had anticipated him coming after her and launched from a run into a two-footed flying kick. Nothing fancy, really just throwing herself at him feet-first, but her now considerable weight and speed turned her from a four foot eleven ninety-pound woman into a quarter ton flying wrecking ball.

Her feet hit Jeffery in the chest, taking him completely by surprise. He let out a shout that was only outdone by the loud cracking of troll ribs. He was lifted off his feet and crashed into a wooden pillar. He caught himself before hitting the ground, fingers digging into the wooden pillar, and splintering it.

Mila somehow kept her balance and was able to follow up the kick with a wild punch that snapped Jeffery's head to the side, his eyes rolling up in his head before he fell flat on his face, out cold.

Mila quickly pulled the golden circlet from his head.

The hounds all stopped, blinking and shaking their heads. Some whined and backed into corners, but all of them assessed the situation as best they could. Mila realized it probably would have been fine, except the Magicals who had holed up behind the bar weren't quick on the uptake and continued to fling offensive spells at the hounds. This set off a chain reaction, and the hounds renewed their attacks. However, this time, they didn't have one person orchestrating their movements; they were all on their own. And nothing is more dangerous than a pack animal hunting with their pack.

The magicals behind the bar were quickly over-whelmed as the hounds moved into a flanking maneuver, coming around and over the sides of the bar. Several more hounds piled onto Finn, and even Penny was suddenly fighting two hounds that were now working together on an instinctual level they had not been able to access while under the circlet's influence.

Mila started to charge towards the bar to help the most vulnerable, but her finger suddenly felt like it was on fire. She slid to a stop and saw that the ring was now smoking, and she felt her stone skin changing at an accelerated rate.

She remembered what Finn had said about it maybe killing her as it tried to pull more power from her, and she quickly pulled the ring off.

Her transformation took much less time than it had the first time since she was already halfway through it as the ring ran out of power. She stumbled back, her weight shifting as she returned to her normal flesh and blood.

She quickly scanned the room but didn't see how she could stop the wild hounds until she felt the circlet in her hands.

"God, Mila," she admonished herself, "if your head wasn't attached, you'd forget you had one."

She lifted the circlet above her head, and after a breath, lowered it to settle over her now black hair.

A sharp spike of pain jumped through her head, and she let out a whimpering scream before her mind was suddenly filled with the thoughts of two dozen wild hell-hounds. The whimper turned into a scream of pain.

She kept focusing on not moving, hoping that it was translating over to the hounds, but she wasn't able to open her eyes to see if it was working. She kept trying to project calm and gentleness through the circlet, and she could feel the circlet rooting through her head, looking for payment for its work. That rooting stopped at the base of her skull, hesitating for a second before latching onto something and sucking hard at it.

She screamed, her hands pressed to her temples. The last thing she felt was her knees hitting the stone floor, then she slid into darkness.

"No!" Finn shouted, seeing Mila lower the circlet onto her head.

Shoving yet another hound from off himself, he struggled to his feet. He was covered in blood from the numerous bites, making him lightheaded from the blood loss. He was finding it hard to hang onto Fragar in his blood-slick hands, but he swung the axe, shattering the hound he had thrown off when it came back around, the axe finally slipping free and clattering to the ground.

He rushed towards Mila, but he heard Penny scream, and a jet of flame caught his attention. He looked to the left and saw that she had been pinned to the ground by two hounds. One of the monsters had taken a bite from her wing, leaving the normally taut skin ragged and bleeding. Penny was flaming them in the face as best she could, but it was ineffective and barely more than a nuisance to her attackers.

He and Penny locked eyes, and he saw something he had never seen there before. Terror.

Finn grabbed a chunk of the shattered hound and threw it at one animal attacking Penny while sprinting in to tackle the second one. The chunk of jagged stone exploded from the impact, making the hound yelp and jump back. He was closing in on the second, but it was already chomping down on Penny's head.

Then the sound of snarling hounds went quiet as every stone skinned beast froze. Finn changed direction, and instead of tackling the hound, he scooped Penny up as gently as he could while still moving fast. He laid her panting body over his shoulder and felt her dig her talons in so as not to fall.

He quickly pointed at the front door, and roared at the remaining stunned bystanders, "Get the fuck out! Now! Move, move!"

The frozen people snapped out of their shocked stupor and all as one made a run for the front door.

Finn spun back to Mila and rushed to her side just as she fell to her knees, her body going limp. He caught her before she could fall all the way to the ground and gently laid her down.

He pulled the circlet from her head and quickly put it on his own head. He channeled pure dwarven power into the artifact, and it sprang to life for him with the ease of turning on a light switch.

The hounds hadn't even twitched as he took control of them. He made them all line up in ranks and sit down at the back of the bar.

He inspected Mila as the rest of the mobile patrons fled out the door. She was out cold and looked peaceful, but when he pulled her hair back, he could see burn marks on her temples—a sure sign she had tried to channel far more power than she had.

"Shiri?" Penny's voice was weak, and she clung to him like a kitten, but her concern was all for Mila.

"I don't know," Finn said. "I hope so."

CHAPTER TWENTY-NINE

The front door burst open and several people in black military uniforms complete with composite armor and helmets on came in in a tight formation, the leading men had rifles of magical design held at the ready as they quickly made sure the room was under control. Several of them stationed themselves around the docile hounds, keeping an eye on them.

Finn saw Hermin and several other Huldu come in after the all-clear was signaled. Danica came in the rear, her bag already open as she snapped on fresh gloves.

"Over here!" Finn called from where he cradled Mila's head in his lap.

Danica spotted him and pushed her way to the front, dropping to her knees beside her friend, and opening one of Mila's eyes and shining a light into it. "What happened to her?" her tone was completely professional and calm.

"She used the circlet to control the hounds for a few seconds. I tried to stop her, but it took me too long to get there." Finn confessed. He pulled back her hair and showed the burns to Danica. They exchanged a look before Danica started taking Mila's vitals. They both knew it wasn't good.

Finn let Danica work and checked on Penny, having her climb down into his arms so he could get a good look at her wing. She cringed with pain but didn't protest as he stretched the bloody appendage to examine it. The bite had gone through the skin between bones; she was lucky in that, but the wound would take a while to heal, so she would not be very mobile.

"Too bad there aren't any healing potions for dragons." He commented, folding her wing back against her body. "But you've recovered from worse. Besides now you can tell people about your bad-ass scar." He smiled at her. She just rolled her eyes.

Glancing around at the controlled chaos of the cleanup, Finn saw several of the military men administering healing both magical and mundane to those who were too injured to get out on their own. He also saw several men locking Jeffery in shackles that had an anti-magical aura that nearly drained the color from the air around them. The troll was still out, but with their accelerated healing, he would be up soon.

Reaching over, he placed a hand on Danica's arm. "I'm going to get these hounds out of here while I have them under control. Will you be okay without me?"

She nodded, not looking up from whatever it was she was mixing in a bowl. "Penny, stay here. I'll have something for that wing in a minute. Plus, I might need your help with our girl here."

Penny patted Finn's arm, pointing to be put down. He

gently lowered her beside Mila, where she sat on her haunches and placed a hand on Mila's forehead.

Knowing there wasn't anything he could do for his two friends, he focused on the things he could do.

Finn stopped the first black-clad trooper he came across and was a little surprised to see that it was a female elf under the helmet. "Who the hell are you people?"

She gave him a roguish smile and tipped her helmet up with a finger. "We're G.A.E.L.," she said, with a hint of pride, tapping the white letters printed on her armor. "Mr. Meriwether brought us in. Too bad we missed the action."

"What the hell does G.A.E.L. stand for?" Finn frowned, trying to guess the acronym.

"Magical defense and concealment league. We do it all." She pointed her rifle at the hounds.

Finn screwed up his face trying to make that work. "That's not how an acronym works. Don't the letters have to match the words?"

"It's from a dead language. We keep trying to have it changed, but there are traditions to uphold. You understand, I'm sure." She pointed her rifle at the hounds. "What are we supposed to do with these, exactly?"

"I'll take care of them." Finn scanned the room. "Is Preston here?"

"I believe he is outside talking with the owner of this establishment. Should I go get him?" she didn't seem all that eager to collect the powerful man.

"That would be great. And be sure to keep the troll here until I get back. I have questions for him."

The elf gave him a salute and jogged out the front door after stopping to say a word to the two troopers keeping an eye on Jeffery. Finn turned to the hounds and, using the circlet and a small burst of magic, made them all stand and turn toward the back door. He had to use a couple of quick spells to free the four hounds he had fused together and the one still stuck in the stone floor, but after a few minutes, he was marching the hounds out into the back alley where the white box truck they had been transported in waited. The back door was still open, so he had the hounds hop up one at a time and lie down. He stepped up onto the rear gate step and pulled the door down, latching it closed. He then sent the hounds a calming signal, soothing their fear and putting the idea of a good night's sleep in their minds before he gently severed the contact.

He was not a master of the device by any means, but his innate ability to use dwarven magic made the process easy for him, where it had obviously been a struggle for Jeffery and had nearly killed Mila.

He returned to find the hulking form of Preston, his human concealment spell firmly in place, squatting beside Danica, Penny, and Mila. The illusion was so good that if Finn hadn't seen a picture of him in a magazine recently, he wouldn't have known who he was.

Preston saw Finn enter and stood to meet him, taking a step away from Danica to let her continue her work, slathering a green paste on Penny's wing.

He held out a large hand to Finn. "This was good work, Finn. I'm sorry we didn't get here in time to help."

Finn shook hands, his bloody hand leaving a red smear on Preston's that the Minotaur didn't seem to notice or care about. "We did what we had to. Help cleaning up is much appreciated, though." He handed the circlet over.

"The hounds are in the truck in the alley. I suggested they take a nap, so they should be easy to transport."

"Thanks for that." He handed the circlet to one of the troopers, who put it in a black cloth sack, and cinched the top closed. "So, you were able to save the hounds as well? That's worth a bonus, for sure. Anita will be pleased."

"I don't know if you should be celebrating or not. You just inherited a pack of magic-resistant hellhounds. I was able to influence them due to my dwarven earth magic, but I saw about two dozen attack spells bounce off of them like they were thrown seaweed."

"We'll be sure to take extra care with them. We may have to put them back into storage. We don't have many stasis chambers still working on this old ship, but we'll find a way."

Preston and Finn turned at the sound of metal clanking and saw that Jeffery had finally recovered enough to wake up. He pulled at the shackles, but they showed no sign of letting loose.

The two large men walked over, staring down at the sitting troll.

"Hey, Jeff." Finn raised an eyebrow. "Turns out you're a real piece of shit, huh?"

Jeffery, for his part, at least had a hint of remorse in his eyes as he surveyed all the victims being treated. Finn noted that at least four of the injured had succumbed to their wounds and were now covered with sheets and being carried out of the building on stretchers.

"I told them it was a bad idea," Jeffery mumbled. "No one listens to the troll, though."

Preston squatted down to be more on his level. "What

was the game plan here? I assume this is all orchestrated by the Dark Star, but what is it she wanted to accomplish?"

"Her plan is simple." Jeffery locked his gaze on his former friend Mila, still lying unconscious a few feet away. "She wants magicals to feel like they don't have anyone looking out for them. If there is enough unrest, they will be willing to fight for protection, and she can swoop in with her promises of a nation of our own. And rights for every race."

Finn laughed entirely too loud. "Oh, now that's a plan right out of dwarven lore if I've ever heard one. Attack the people in secret so they come to you for protection. Are we sure I'm the only dwarf left on *Earth*?"

"It sounds crude, but I'm afraid it's working." Preston sighed. "There have been reports all over the globe of things like this happening. Most communities don't have someone like me to guide them, so they flock to the first thing that looks like safety."

"And in most places, that's a Dark Star agent?" Finn guessed. Preston nodded. "Okay, I can understand the attacks in a twisted way as a good idea for her organization, but why did you send assassins after us? You had to know we wouldn't be taken out that easily." Finn asked Jeffery, who cocked his head to the side in confusion.

"What assassins?"

Finn narrowed his eyes. "The one you sent after Mila and me at the hospital? Then the ones you sent to Preston's estate?"

He shook his head. "I didn't have anything to with that. How would I get assassins onto one of the best-guarded estates in the country?"

"Then who was it?" Finn asked, raising an eyebrow.

"Why should I tell you?"

Preston stood and took a step forward, his large bulk suddenly looming. "Because if you do, I can put in a good word for you. No matter what happens with the Dark Star, you'll never be a part of it now. But I can make your time in prison easier. Call it "going state's evidence" if you like. Who knows, you might even get your own shower."

Jeffery was, evidently, not a stupid troll. He took about three seconds to consider before spilling the beans. "I only talked with him once, and it was on the phone, but I heard that Kashgar son of a bitch in charge call him Kal multiple times."

Finn looked over to see Preston's expression go dark for a second before he smiled at Jeffery. "Thank you. I'll be sure you are treated well in your new home." He turned and immediately pulled a phone from his pocket, hitting a speed dial number.

"Is she all right?" Jeffery asked, true concern in his voice.

Finn looked away from Preston and saw Jeffery gazing at the prone form of Mila. Finn took a second to process the feelings that seeing her lying there caused his blood to boil in his chest before answering.

"I don't know. Physically, she should be fine. Dr. Meadows got her to drink a healing potion, so the damage is now purely magical. Physically she'll recover, but I have no idea what you did to her peabrain. Only time will tell."

Jeffery swallowed hard. "I tried to keep her away from all this. She has something special about her that I never understood." He looked up at Finn. "Do you know about her affinity for insects? I've never seen anything like it. I never found a trace of magic in her, but she could still communicate with them. It's an indication of much more, but I'll be damned if I can tell what it is."

Two of the G.A.E.L. troopers came over and lifted Jeffery up to his feet, keeping a tight hold on his shackled arms, preparing to take him away.

"Tell her I'm sorry." He frowned, his face hardening. "I'm not sorry that the attack went forward, just how it turned out. And that she had to pay for it. The Dark Star isn't wrong, just her methods might be flawed, but we magicals need a place we can call home. Look around, dwarf. You'll see that I'm right."

The troopers pulled him towards the door, Jeffery going without a fight. Finn watched them go, noting Jeffery never took his eyes off of Mila. He was pretty sure there were tears in the troll's eyes by the time he was out the door.

"He's gone." Preston rumbled, turning back to Finn and putting his phone in his suit pocket.

"Kal? Yeah, I figured he would be in the wind by now. That attack on us in your office was a desperate move that brought too much heat down on him. He had to know it was only a matter of time before you found him out." Finn stepped closer to Mila, watching Danica finish up with Penny by wrapping her injured wing tight against her body with white gauze, leaving the other free. "What's your plan?"

Preston sighed, scratching at his square chin. "I made a mistake with the Dark Star. I assumed she was just another fanatic with visions of grandeur, but it turns out that she's got a well-funded organization with visions of grandeur, which is a much more formidable position. The fact that she had someone as close to me as Kal was speaks of a network with deep resources."

"Worse than that." Finn turned to meet the Minotaur's eyes, "Her message isn't wrong. In the last few days, we've met a fair number of groups that need what she's selling. They need a place to exist that isn't shrouded from the world. Places like the Menagerie and the Markets are great and all, but they're tiny islands in the vast sea of humanity. Take the advice of a dwarf whose father basically rules the universe; people need a place to belong to and call their own. The common man will put up with a lot of shit if he can go to a home and say, 'this is mine.' You've done pretty well in taking care of your people here in Denver, but there's a big world out there, and most of those people don't have a Preston Meriwether looking out for them."

Preston narrowed his eyes as if seeing Finn for the first time. "What would you suggest we do, Dwarf King?"

Finn waved off the comment. "How should I know? I'm just an exiled traveler trying to find a place to call home myself." He looked down at Mila. Penny stood beside her, gently stroking her hair and cooing a soft dragon song to her. "I do know one thing for certain." He looked at Preston, who was giving him his full attention. "I'm no king. Hell, if you ask my father, I'm barely a dwarf. I'll leave the ruling to those better suited to it."

"You're an Earthling now. The past is out there." He waved a hand at the ceiling and the sky beyond. "But the future is here on this broken-down ship we call home. If there is one thing I know for certain, it's that the future is unknowable. Don't sell yourself short, Finn. People might just need what you've thrown away. I've found that the best leaders are the ones who don't want it but understand the costs."

Danica put a hand on his shoulder, turned him her way, and held out a roll of bandages. "Give me your arms. I'm going to wrap you up until we get home and I can get a healing potion in you. I need yours for some of the others." He held out his arms, and she began wrapping them with expert hands. She finished quickly, took his two healing potions, and nodded to him before heading off to help others.

Finn frowned. He didn't like to think about what it meant to be Finnegan Dragonbender, the son of the king, and what that position meant. He just wanted to be Finn. He wanted to help his friend find her hoard. He wanted to have people that understood the call of adventure and could revel in it with him. He wanted a tribe to call his own.

He wanted Mila to...he wasn't sure what he wanted from her. That wasn't true, he realized; he knew exactly what he wanted from her. He also knew she deserved better than an exiled berserker dwarf. She deserved a prince.

As if thinking of her had triggered something in her brain, Mila's eyes fluttered open.

Finn fell to his knees beside her, helping her to sit up with a hand on her back. "How are you feeling? You gave us quite the scare." Finn spoke softly, his voice sounding more worried than he had realized he had been.

She groaned and gripped the back of her neck,

massaging the base of her skull. "I feel like a demolition derby had a full tournament in my head." She smiled and looked up into his face. "It's a good thing you and Penny owe me a two-hour massage."

Finn barked a laugh, his fear escaping with it. "I thought it was half an hour."

"Not after this shit." She held out her arms to him like a child. "Pick me up."

He leaned in, and she wrapped her arms around his neck. He cradled her to his chest. "Let's get you home."

She nodded into his chest. "That sounds good."

CHAPTER THIRTY

Mila slept for the next three days, only waking long enough to eat a lazy meal and go to the bathroom before she returned to the couch and inevitably fell back asleep, laying her head on either Finn's or Danica's lap. Even when the loud banging and power saws of construction started on the condo next door, she slept.

Finn would watch as Danica took Mila's vitals then performed a check on her magical aura, but like each time before, there was nothing to see.

Penny was recovering quickly. Her natural healing ability grew back the missing skin of her wing in just over a day and a half, even though it wouldn't be thick enough to support her weight for a few more days. She had removed the bandages, complaining that she was far too itchy to leave them on. Danica had finally relented, allowing her to remove the gauze only to end up staring with wide eyes at the healed-over wound, never having seen a dragon's rapid healing abilities before then.

Finn, for his part, made food when it was time, or went

over plans with the construction team next door to make sure they had everything they needed to get the project done quickly, but mostly he sat on the couch watching John Wayne movies while acting as a pillow for Mila. He had to give Danica credit for acting as a backup pillow and/or footrest while sitting through seventeen westerns, and one mistake of a bad movie about Genghis Khan.

So, on the third night, when Mila awoke, rubbing the sleep from her eyes, and declared that she really wanted to go out for a drink and to sing some karaoke, Finn and Danica jumped at the opportunity. Even Penny was excited to get out of the house, and she had been the least bored of them all, using her time to surf the web and buy who-knew-what with the company's new credit card.

"Wait, he just gave you the ring?" Mila asked, taking a sip of her G&T while snatching a honey-roasted peanut from the bowl Penny was lounging in.

They had taken a table near the small stage at the front of the Refinery. Finn, Mila, and Penny were sipping their drinks while Danica serenaded the small weekday crowd with a soulful rendition of *Black Velvet*.

"He said it was a bonus for keeping all but one of the hounds alive, and for going in without backup from his strike team." Finn snatched one of the peanuts as well, but Penny took a swipe at him, although she had pretended not to notice when Mila had done the same. "Said there would be plenty more work if we wanted it, too. Not a bad idea to have a billionaire indebted to us, especially since we know the Dark Star is going to be making herself better known."

"So that's the plan? Hunt down the Dark Star?"

Finn nodded, then shook his head. "I don't know yet. To be honest, I think we need to do some serious thinking about what it is the Dark Star is trying to do. She has a plan, and after hearing what Jeffery had to say, I can't blame people for following her. People need a place to belong where they can be themselves."

"I feel like defeating the Dark Star wouldn't really solve the problem, then. Without her, the disenfranchised will just flock to the next opportunity. That's what happened in Russia after the Czar was killed, and it didn't turn out great for a lot of their people. I can't even imagine what that would look like on a global scale."

"I'm not sure what a Russia or a Czar is, but I think I get your drift. Something similar happened to one of my father's provinces." Finn said, his brows furrowing at the memory.

"How did he solve the problem?" Mila asked, sneaking another peanut while Penny looked away in an obvious attempt to seem oblivious.

A dark look passed over Finn's face. "He killed them."

"The people heading up the coup?"

Finn shook his head. "No. He killed them all. I did mention my father was a monster, right?"

The look of horror on Mila's face was all Finn needed to see to know that a subject change was on the table. "That's why we need a plan. I want to start asking magicals what it is they need; see if there is a simpler solution to the problem."

She nodded, taking a sip of her drink. "That's not a bad plan. We need to get the lay of the land before we can work to change it."

He gave her a smile. "That's what I love about you; you always assume we're going to succeed."

Mila rubbed at the back of her neck, closing her eyes as a bit of pain reared up.

"You okay?" Finn had been a little on edge over her condition ever since they arrived.

She nodded and gave him a smile. "Yeah. Just a little residual stiffness. Nothing a song or two won't cure." She slipped off her stool, and leaned against him, resting her head on his shoulder. "Thanks for taking care of me, but don't think you're getting out of your bet. You still owe me an hour-long foot massage."

Finn cocked his head at her as if she were crazy. "I have been rubbing your feet and your shoulders and back and anything else you presented to me over the last three days. I figured you would be a massaged to a fine paste by now."

She shook her head, her face completely serious. "It didn't count."

"Why not?"

"Because I don't remember it. I must have been asleep." She shrugged, giving him a mockingly sad face. "Sorry, but you still owe me."

He smiled, putting an arm around her shoulders. "I'll be happy to fulfill my end of the bargain."

She stood on her tiptoes and gave him a peck on the cheek. "I know." She turned and sauntered off towards the stage just as Danica finished up to a round of applause.

Finn watched her go, a grin plastered on his face. She

stopped and turned back her brows furrowed. "Wait. What exactly did I "present" for a rubdown while I was out of it?"

His brows began to creep up his forehead, but before he had to answer, she burst out laughing and skipped up onto the stage, smacking Danica on the butt as she passed her.

Finn glanced down at Penny, who was doing her best not to laugh, but making eye contact with him was more than the little dragon could take. She huffed a ball of smoke out as she snorted a laugh before clamping a hand over her mouth.

"You know as well as I do that nothing happened." He rolled his eyes, which made Penny laugh all the more.

"What's so funny?" Danica asked, taking Mila's stool and reaching across the table for her glass of white wine.

"Nothing." Finn grumped as Penny held up her hands and squeezed the air while doing a pretty good impression of a honking horn.

Danica raised an eyebrow at the display. "You know what? I don't think I want to know."

Mila started her song—*With a Little Help from My Friends,* the Joe Cocker version. They listened as she sang the first verse, her eyes closed when she hit the high notes. The crowd loved her commitment if not her skill.

"So, what do you think?" Finn asked, leaning in and speaking low so they weren't overheard.

"About the song? Solid choice." Danica tapped her fingers on the table along with the beat.

"It is a good choice, but I was talking about her condition."

Danica turned to look at him, a frown on her face. "I honestly don't know yet. She burned herself out good with that damned thing. Honestly, I'm surprised she's out of bed. I figured she would sleep for a good couple of weeks."

"It was that bad?" Finn had known it wasn't good, but Danica hadn't made that big a deal out of it. Now he realized she hadn't said anything for Mila's benefit.

Danica nodded. "If it were a magical this had happened to, I would say they would be cut off from their magic forever. Their magical center would have been burned up for good. But along with that, they would have never woken from their coma as she has, so she's already defying the odds." She turned and watched Mila for a few seconds, a faraway look on her face. "There's something different about our girl. I give it fifty-fifty odds she is either cut off from magic forever or that it comes back and is stronger than ever. I just don't know."

A buzz made Finn look down at the table, and he noticed Mila had left her phone. The screen lit up with the name Preston Meriwether.

"You going to get that?" Danica asked, her eyes wide at the thought of one of the most powerful men in the country having her friend's personal number.

Finn sighed. "I really don't want too. I just want to have a nice quiet night with my friends." He picked up the phone anyway and hit the accept button. "Hello?"

"Finn." Preston didn't sound surprised it was him. "You really need to get a phone."

"I have one."

"True, but it isn't doing you much good since it was buried with Peter's body when no one came to claim his things."

Finn shrugged. "I don't know. It's saved me from having to use it. What can we do for you, Preston?"

"It's not what you can do for me, but what I can do for you." He paused for dramatic effect, which made Finn roll his eyes.

"Okay, I'll bite. What can you do for me?" Finn said, downing the rest of his mostly full whiskey.

"I can tell you where the *Anthem* is."

Finn, Penny and Mila are working as a team, but the cost of victory is mounting. The Dark Star has taken the Anthem and is rebuilding the ship. Finn wants to get it back but it's at the bottom of a lake and Dwarves hate water. They sink fast.

Plus, there's that price on his head.

Join Finn and his friends in their next adventure as they face the Dark Star once and for all in Anthem of the Dwarf King*!*

Get sneak peeks, exclusive giveaways, behind the scenes content, and more.
PLUS you'll be notified of special **one day only fan pricing** on new releases.

Sign up today to get free stories.

CLICK HERE

or visit: https://marthacarr.com/read-free-stories/

First off, thanks for reading the book. Just the fact that you picked it up and gave it a chance means the world to me. Seriously.

I never know what to write in these notes. I always figure my fiction words are what people are after, so why bore them with the personal stuff?

Then I remember that storytelling is personal. As an author, my job is to keep the story going in an interesting and fun way, but I'll let you all in on a little secret.

Most of us don't have any clue what we're doing.

Now, I don't mean that we don't know how to twist a sentence to make it sound better. Or that we don't understand the power of a comma (Let's eat grandma! Let's eat, grandma!).

No, when I say we don't know what we're doing, what I mean is, we don't know what it's like to be other people. No one does.

But in my books, there are hundreds of different characters, each one with hopes and dreams of their own, but they also all have one thing in common; me. Each one of them has a little piece of me in their DNA, and if you know what parts to pick out you could stitch together a pretty good facsimile of my life.

Everything is in there. How I felt when I lost my shoe in the Thames river when I was nine. The first girl I ever kissed. How a popsicle tasted on the hottest day of the year on my grandparents' farm in Ohio. The day I married my wife. The day my father died.

It's all there in tiny bits and pieces, right out in the open but also scattered over a hundred lives.

It's late and the cats are passed out on the cat tree in my office. They all have their own spot, all curled up in a hammock or on a plush bed; it's a really nice cat tree. My wife has gone to bed, humoring me while I write to my friends, but still a little pissed that I didn't get this done earlier. I told her I didn't know what to say.

"Don't you write for a living?" She cocked a brow and narrowed her eyes.

"Yeah. But that's different. I make that stuff up."

She laughed. "No you don't. You just adapt stuff from your real life. I've read your books, honey. I know where you got it from."

"Well, shit... you're right."

My wife is smarter than me.

I love you all, and I'll see you in the next book. (and if you know where to look, you'll see me there too)

Charley Case

(December 5th, 2019
Boise, Idaho)

Want to connect with me? Follow me on Facebook or join my Facebook group.

I first met Ramy Vance at 20Books50k convention in 2018. He was yelling out my name from down a long, wide hallway. "Martha Carr! Martha Carr! I want to be you!" It was his enthusiasm that kept me from running the other way and fading into the crowd. It's his best characteristic. He leads with joy and curiosity. Except for that time I drove us both over a wall... It was dark, okay? And Ramy said nothing about that wall I didn't see. Besides, as I told him, it's a Subaru. They can take it. Best part was Ramy muttering, "Good thing we know a cop." And when I gunned it to get the car over the rest of the way, I saw (and it's the only time I've seen it) a genuine look of fear on his face and he said, resigned to our fate, "Oh, he can't help us now..."

But, it was a Subaru... No damage, no problems. We laughed so hard it was a while before I could drive again. And yes, I was still doing the driving. Did I mention we were out at night looking for a commercial vacuum to suck up the broken glass from where someone had broken in while we were at dinner? That's what it's like with Ramy.

Every encounter is an adventure. I swear, my life is serene until the literary whirlwind blows in and we head out there again looking for fun that usually finds us. Till we meet again, Ramy. I'll go gas up the car.

Martha Carr

1. What turns you on?

Would it be crass of me to admit it's … Ahh, I mean, humor. A great sense of humor turns me on…

2. What turns you off?

Someone who makes a big deal out of everything.

3. Who do you most admire? Why?

My mom because, at the age of 68, she picked up and started over. Truly inspiring.

4. What profession other than your own would you like to attempt?

Professional Video Game Tester … that's a thing, right?

5. What profession would you not like to do?

Accountant. Unless it's for the mob.

6. If heaven exists, what would you like to hear God say when you arrive at the pearly gates?

Gone, eh? (You'll get that if you've read my GoneGod series.)

7. What is your favorite movie?

At age 10 – Highlander. At age 40 – Highlander.

8. Who is your favorite character and from what book by which author?

Hazel from Watership Down.

9. What is something most people do not know about you?

I used to be a champion show-horse rider.

10. What do you look forward to most in the new year?

Publishing 20 books in my universe

11. What's your favorite non-LMBPN series you've done? What's your favorite series inside LMBPN?

GoneGod World (out of it). Middang3ard inside LMBPN.

12. Do you have a web site you'd like to promote?

www.paradise-lot.com

OTHER BOOKS IN THE TERRANAVIS UNIVERSE

The Adventures of Maggie Parker Series

The Witches of Pressler Street

Other books by Martha Carr

Other books by Charley Case

JOIN THE TERRANAVIS UNIVERSE FACEBOOK GROUP

FOLLOW TERRANAVIS UNIVERSE ON FACEBOOK